Bridger's diary: A Mozart fantasy

By David Spiller

Copyright © 2020 by David Spiller

Also by David Spiller:

Pilot Error

Out of Burma

Girl at Dunkirk

Five years in India

(Available on Amazon)

Bridger's diary: A Mozart fantasy

Introduction by Kate Temple

Larry Bridger's diary, scrawled in an unlined notebook, was found shortly after his death in 2065. It was amongst mounds of books in his apartment in New York, where he had emigrated to from Britain 30 years earlier. The diary was obviously written for Bridger's private use and it is unlikely anyone else has seen it. Until now.

Bridger's modest reputation as a writer means that his name is not particularly well known in the UK. The diary merits publication because it sheds light, albeit briefly, on a much more famous individual: the British composer, Martin Amade. Bridger began writing in 2035, around the time of his first meeting with the composer, kept it up for a year – the last year of Amade's life – then stopped abruptly.

Amade was known in British music circles, but when the diary began 30 years ago few would have predicted his future status as one of the greatest composers ever to grace the planet. Yet Bridger perhaps divined some inkling of this and felt it worth putting his thoughts on paper. The publishers of the diary are glad he did. Readers must judge for themselves their importance.

As well as providing invaluable information on Amade the diary also records some lurid details of Bridger's personal life. My first thought on reading him was that Bridger belonged amongst autobiographers like Benvenuto Cellini and Axel Munthe; that is, as one of the greatest liars in literature. After editing his diary I've come to believe the man usually told the truth – so long as one accepts some exaggeration of his amorous exploits.

Mindful of a lamentable decline in scholarship over recent decades, I have checked whatever facts can be checked and appended some notes at the end of each daily record, where they should be easily accessible to readers. I have not made any cuts to the diary; Bridger's original text, with all its scurrilous detail, is exactly as I found it.

Nor have I made any analysis of the cataclysmic changes in our planet and our lives during the 30-year period after Bridger's diary ends. That is another story entirely.

Kate Temple, October 2066

The diary

March 23, 2035

Well hello diary! I've decided to write down bits of my life in a journal, and I may as well start today. I see it as an alternative to the psychiatrist's couch, which I can't afford. I hope I don't disappear up my own arse whilst writing the thing.

Dear God, what a time I had yesterday. My head's still whirling. One interesting point was that I met the composer Martin Amade. But for much of the time my mind was elsewhere, as I shall now relate.

It was a Monday, and I had my usual Monday arrangement with a young married woman called Tracey. We always met in the centre of Brum (**Ref 1**), had a meal out, then went back to my place. Nice. Trace and I been meeting on Mondays for several months and she seemed happy enough with the arrangement. She said it jollied up the worst day of the week. I did remember later that she'd once looked a bit wistful and complained she was only my Monday girl. Note the 'only'. Perhaps I should listen to people more carefully.

Tracey runs this old Mini which she feeds with illegal petrol. There are supplies all over the city if you know where to look. Of course that is illegal too, but the authorities take no notice. Nobody thinks about the future, only the here and now. There's a crazy mood abroad that combines resignation and febrile excitement. Anyway, we'd had a half-decent meal and Tracey drove nimbly, darting between the electric vehicles and the usual hordes of bicycles. She wore a polka dot dress and I had one hand under the hem. I felt at peace with the world – but not for long. Without any warning she looked across the front seat of the car in a strange way, almost running over a stray goat in the process.

'I've done it,' she said.

'Done what?' My mind was on other things.

'My husband. I've told him – about us.'

'You *what*!'

'Well not *told* him, exactly. I left a note. He'll find it any moment now. It describes the situation – you know, I've met someone else, I don't want to be with him any more, that kind of thing.'

For a moment I was stunned. A cold hand twisted my vital organs, rearranging things down there. Tracey's husband was a builder and those guys don't mess about.

Then, '*Turn the car round*! *Turn round*, god damn it.'

She looked puzzled but did what I said, and we returned to her apartment at the double. Inside she found that her note hadn't been disturbed and came back with the glad tidings. Of course that wasn't the end of it – or rather, that *was* the end, after an hour of tearful recriminations. Monday afternoons were no more. I know I shall feel the ache of their absence for months.

The incident disturbed me more than I'd thought possible, because I went straight back to my grotty bedsit and tried to analyse what I felt in this diary. I tried to see things her way. But my case for the defence is simple. When I told Tracey 'I love you', I really meant it. I'm the same with other girls, or I wouldn't say it. Maybe some guys aren't as sincere in these situations, but I am and I think that should count for something.

Now about the Martin Amade moment. I had it noted on my phone to call in at the Electric for 7.30. Because my living is writing for the stage, I have to keep up with live theatre. For three nights the Electric was running some play about a fire that decimated a garment factory in a New York tenement. It sounded unpromising but my thinking was – first half hour, toe in the water, then skedaddle. I got to the Electric on time and settled into a seat at the back, so I could slip out unobtrusively.

The old place had seen better days and showed signs of its former existence as a cinema. (**Ref 2**) I suppose it was a third full, which is good going in the present climate. Of course I was in a bad mood; sad about Tracey and sluggish from thwarted desire. My expectations were low.

In one way the evening turned out as expected. The play was a poor thing. I soon saw how it could be improved because the writer – someone unknown to me – hadn't mastered his craft. The plot creaked and the characters lacked all conviction. Normally I'd have been out of there pronto.

Instead of which I remained glued to my seat. To my own surprise the reason was the music. I'd not even known there *was* music, but yes – the characters sang all right, individually and in groups, and were supported by half a dozen instrumentalists. No doubt about who was in charge of them. A bloke conducted from the keyboard, and it was clear from his passionate mannerisms that this was Martin Amade, who the programme said was responsible for the music.

Never has a man's appearance so belied his achievements. The fellow was in his early 30s, small (maybe 5 feet 4) and quite podgy, physically unprepossessing with sallow skin and a great clump of mousy hair. The only feature of note was a colourful waistcoat that didn't match the rest of him. But his music... I was transfixed, which was odd because I've never been much into music. I'm not tone deaf or whatever, but I always think – why listen to notes when there are so many wonderful, wonderful words to be devoured. Maybe this attitude is the result of circumstances; the music for these one-off events is generally pretty naff. The songs ape the numbers from more famous shows, the rhythms are very basic, there are few decent melodies, and so on.

But this Electric affair was completely different. The entire musical score was organic – even I could tell – with each bit developing from another bit, and then another, and the whole infused with a piercing melancholy that was entirely right for the subject. I felt like paraphrasing Miranda in *The tempest*, crying out 'O brave new world that has such music in it'. And all this for a minor show running for three nights in a clapped-out fleapit. The play didn't remotely warrant such a seductive score, but it was as if the nondescript little chap in the waistcoat *couldn't bring himself* to write the naff music it deserved. Part of me thought 'Mr Amade you're wasting your talent'; another part was brimming over with admiration.

Against my usual practice I stayed to the very end of the show. When the scruffy little composer took his bow I found that I'd risen to my feet shouting 'encore'. In the next row a theatre critic who knew me stared in amazement.

If I'm known for anything it's my sudden inspirations. Preparing to leave the theatre, I felt another epiphany on the way. I would meet up with this Amade fellow and propose that we cooperate on a show – my words, his music – and this time both components would be of the highest quality. His career stood to gain as much as mine. I went into the lobby jaunty with anticipation and asked a staff member where I could find Martin Amade.

'You can't,' she said.

'I beg your pardon!'

'Mr Amade isn't well. I have the strictest instructions not to let anyone in to see him.'

I gave this woman the once-over, covertly of course. She was slight in build but looked determined.

'Suppose I write a note that you could take to him?' I said. 'I intend to suggest a way we could work together. It would be to his advantage, I promise.'

She gave a grim smile. 'Mr Amade is besieged with proposals for collaboration. Several of his so-called *partners*' – she spat the word out – 'Have taken advantage of him.'

I never push against a closed door. I thanked her and went on my way, no matter. My life has been festooned with inspirations that failed to take root. My favourable impression of Amade's music will fade, I reassured myself. Besides, I already have three writing commitments lined up, admittedly none of them worth the candle.

I stepped out of the theatre onto the pavement. The time was exactly ten o'clock. A look up and down the street confirmed that a mere smattering of people were about, a fraction of the Brum nite-life that would have flourished ten years earlier. Most of those I saw were men or people in groups; these days not too many women trip about after dark. It's different for me. I can handle most situations that might arise. I carry a knife, but only as a last resort.

In my defence – given what happened next – I still felt unsettled by what had transpired earlier in the day. An image of Tracey with no clothes on had been dangled before my eyes and snatched away again. I knew sleep wouldn't come easily that night. And then a woman who'd emerged from the theatre brushed past me on the pavement, leaving a trace of perfume in the air, and this simple action sparked my brain into gear.

An actress of my acquaintance lived a 5-minute walk away and I happened to know that her partner worked late; I knew because he was in a late-night cabaret that I'd written. No sooner the thought than the deed. My feet were already dancing along the paving stones.

She lived in a terraced house on a side street. A light shone in her front room. The curtains were drawn but a gap in the middle revealed Ava crossing the room in a loose-fitting robe. The very sight strengthened my resolve. I hung back for a moment or two in case anyone else showed, then tapped on the front door. There was a pause, during which I knew she was scrutinising her unexpected visitor from a side window, then the door opened.

'*Larry?*'

'The same.'

'I thought it was you. Jake's not here I'm afraid.'

'I hoped he wouldn't be.'

'What!' She was puzzled for a moment, then annoyed. 'Oh no!
You've got a nerve. Looming out of the night like this. I've not seen you
for months.'

'Ava, have a heart.'

'Go away.'

The door was partly ajar – enough for me to reach out and put a hand
inside her robe. Her warm, soft breast was the most wonderful feeling
in the world.

'God damn it!' She pulled me inside and shut the door. I knew her,
you see. I knew that she'd once turned up at *my* door in a similar way. I
knew that she was always randy. And maybe – who knows – she and
Jake were having one of those cool periods in their love life. That
wasn't my business. What mattered was that she was there – and now I
was too.

She led the way through the house. It was a long thin affair with a
corridor coming off the front room, then a kitchen, then a lounge that
looked onto a small back garden. She pulled a drape across the French
window.

'You've got a nerve,' she said again.

One of Ava's little ways was to make love devoid of all clothes and
ornaments, and oblige her partner to follow suit. She let her robe slip
to the floor and removed a bracelet from her wrist and four or five rings
from her fingers. My own clothes got thrown behind the sofa. Only the
sight of my shoes, discarded by the French window, suggested that I
hadn't arrived at the house stark naked. Ava was already squirming on

the sofa. It looked as if she'd put on a bit of weight. I started to make a move but she raised a hand and pointed.

'Oi! Socks.'

'Oh! Of course. Sor-*ree*.'

We set to it. But now I was to find, big time, that it *really* wasn't my day. Ava had barely started to whisper 'Yes, that's nice,' when we heard the front door opening, She was up like a scolded cat.

'Oh Christ! It's Jake.'

She had the robe back on before my bum left the sofa, then swept up all her jewellery in one hand. She's done this before, I thought. We could hear Jake moving through the house towards us, discovery imminent. Now she had the French window open and was waving me urgently through it.

'My clothes,' I hissed, but she shook her head violently and motioned towards the garden. What could a man do? Out I went, grabbing my shoes on the way. The night air struck my body and the French window closed behind me. I heard a muted version of her greeting, welcoming her partner home like any good little woman. 'Back early, darling?' were the opening words. God's teeth! What a work of art is woman.

I looked up to take in my immediate surroundings. I was in a small garden bounded by fences on three sides. Overhead the moon was inconveniently bright, illuminating every blade of grass on Ava's lawn. My instinct was to move away from the house, not least because scuffling sounds and a creaking sofa suggested Jake was finishing the job I'd started. A little squeak came from Ava, damn her. I stooped to get my shoes on, then flitted across the lawn. I'd absolutely no idea what to do. Climbing one of the side fences would merely get me into someone else's garden. The back fence looked more promising, with a communal passageway visible behind, but it was head high and presented a more serious obstacle. What now? Nearby was a rubbish bin, a rusted metal affair that belonged to the dark ages. I pulled it towards the fence, clambered up and began to scramble over the top. For one dreadful moment I thought my scrotum had become impaled on a protruding nail. But I broke free and fell in a heap the other side. There was a clunk as the lid of the rubbish bin fell off. A dog barked nearby.

Of course my troubles were only beginning. The pathway, running behind half a dozen houses, was easy enough to negotiate, though weeds had grown untended and a clump of stinging nettles savaged my backside. I emerged onto a road with flats on either side. There was the usual inadequate street lighting, and people's reluctance to venture out at night now worked to my advantage. All the same I would never get back to my bedsit, a 20-minute walk away, without meeting somebody. Sure enough a passing cyclist gave a falsetto whoop at the sight of my bare arse. And after I'd crept a few more yards in the shadows a couple emerged from their front door and stood gaping in astonishment.

'Bloody hell,' said the bloke. 'What've we got here?'

I told him 'Sorry mate – doing it for a bet.'

Luckily they were the sort to be amused rather than shocked. I noticed the woman taking a good look. As they walked away she said 'They always look so small, don't they.'

This incident put the seal on my lousy day. But the brain is a curious organ, and its activities are unpredictable. What now passed through my mind was a musical work I'd heard years before in Italy. I'd no recollection of who wrote the thing, but in this work a notorious libertine goes through the entire plot pursuing different women without ever getting his end away. It seemed that I'd managed something similar today. (**Ref 3**)

Worse was to follow. I was still wondering how to find some cover when three men approached on my side of the street. I *heard* the buggers first since they were in high spirits, laughing and joking, kicking up a rare din. I looked round wildly, noticed a waist-high kiosk that normally contained advertising circulars, and slipped behind it. It struck me that one of the men resembled Martin Amade, the music maestro at the Electric theatre. I wasn't sure because he wore a cape concealing the egregious green waistcoat, but the same short stature and podgy frame, the same bunch of mousy hair...it had to be him. So much for his being unwell; the man was clearly in rude health, as he proceeded to demonstrate. One of the others called out 'Martin, you gay dog' and the composer cried 'I am indeed a gay dog' and started barking in high-pitched yelps, bounding about the pavement raising his hands like paws. In a trice the other two had magicked a trumpet and a piccolo from somewhere on their persons to play a frenetic melody that only encouraged the composer's antics. Now Amade bounded up to a street lamp and cocked his leg, laughing like a hyena. The contrast between this mad clowning and his impassioned demeanour in the Electric theatre was astonishing. Still unaware of my presence the two instrumentalists now said their goodbyes (actually, sang them) and crossed the road to turn down a street opposite. Amade continued on to where I stood cowering behind the kiosk. He'd have ignored me – a sensible precaution in Brum around midnight – had I not spoken.

'Um...Mr Amade?'

'Do we know each other?' He'd paused a cautious distance away.

'Not exactly. I saw your show this evening.'

He took a second look at my naked figure. 'Was it too hot in the theatre?' he asked, with another blast of hyena laughter.

'No, er...something else happened afterwards. The thing is...I thought your music was wonderful. It was a revelation.'

'Oh yes, it was far too good for that show,' he said, entirely without false modesty (**Ref 4**). 'No matter. I'm used to it.'

He made to walk on, but again I detained him. 'Look, I'm a writer,' I said hastily. 'I've written several plays for the Birmingham stage. Larry Bridger.'

'I'm sorry – I've not come across the name.'

'No, I understand. But I'm a good writer. I am, really. What I wondered is...do you think we might write something together? My words, your music. I have a plot in mind – something based on a turn-of-the-century novel.'

'I see. Have you any experience of writing a libretto for music?'

'No, none at all.'

Amade peered again, though he couldn't have made out much in the darkness. Of course I realised it was hopeless, raising a subject like that in such absurd circumstances; it surprised me he hadn't taken to his heels already. Or so I thought, but then it happened. I heard him say 'We could discuss it if you like. I live in the Moseley area. Would you be able to call tomorrow? Say around mid-day?'

'Oh!' I spluttered a reply. 'Yes of course. Thank you. Thank you.'

He gave his address, then took the cape from his shoulders and handed it over. 'Perhaps you'd be good enough to return this when you come.'

And before I could say a proper thank-you he was gone.

I donned the cape myself and began the walk to my bedsit, thinking about this bizarre encounter. Amade had met a naked stranger in the street and invited him home the following day, no questions asked. His only concern seemed to be the chance – and an unlikely one at that – of cooperating on some work. It was unusual, to say the least. Not many men would have done as he did.

References

(Ref 1) *At this stage of his much-travelled life Bridger was living in Birmingham, a place he usually referred to as 'Brum'.*

(Ref 2) *The Electric Cinema opened in Birmingham's Station Street in 1909 and at one time claimed to be the oldest working cinema in Britain. It stopped showing films in 2029 and after a while became a venue for amateur or semi-professional theatre groups. Later a preservation order was placed upon the building, which was nevertheless pulled down in 2053.*

(Ref 3) *The work Bridger remembered seeing was probably the opera 'Don Giovanni', music by Wolfgang Amadeus Mozart, libretto by Lorenzo da Ponte. It was first performed in 1787.*

(Ref 4) *Amade's self-confident appraisal of his own music was typical of the man's whole career. The composer knew the extent of his genius, though it took the rest of the world decades to catch up. His forthright attitude sometimes caused offence, though Bridger – with a well-developed ego of his own – seemed barely to have noticed it.*

March 24, 2035

I woke late this morning, and the events of the previous evening seemed more like a dream than real life. Had I really waltzed naked through the streets of central Birmingham? Had I, in that condition, asked a reputable composer to do some work with me? It seemed unlikely, but I had a scrap of paper with a scrawled note to myself – 'Martin Amade, mid-day', and then an address in Moseley – so I gulped down a cup of coffee and hurried out to find a bus.

I was lucky. Public transport is notoriously unreliable – not to say dirty, and sometimes dangerous – but I reached Moseley without incident on top of a double-decker. I'd not been to the place for donkey's years and it was in quite a state. I alighted in the centre by a triangular patch of land where steps led down to a gents toilet, an antique establishment, locked and bolted, that hadn't heard the patter of piss for many a decade. Next to it a couple of wooden benches where residents used to sit and stare were now just about visible through a tangle of undergrowth. Vagrants were on the scene, as blankets and scraps of flapping canvas testified. Rubbish lay thickly in the gutters. The surrounding streets, which once featured numerous retail outlets and cafés, were now dominated by boarded-up shop fronts and broken window panes. Amidst this scene of desecration the occasional convenience store contrived a limp existence. A sprinkling of Moseley citizens moved warily along the broken paving stones. An old bloke stood stock still to stare down a drain.

I checked my scrap of paper for Amade's address and pushed on to a grim area that soon had me looking over my shoulder for trouble. I was wearing Amade's cape, and the glaring mid-day sun brought sweat springing from every pore. The whole enterprise seemed like a wild goose chase – until I spotted a terraced house corresponding to the required address.

The frontage of this place was so old, the woodwork so splintered and decayed, that I double-checked the door number. But the windows contained yellowing net curtains that might conceivably conceal inhabitants, and above my head one of the windows was open, permitting the toxic street air to filter inside. I swallowed hard and rapped my knuckles against the front door. Flakes of paintwork detached themselves and drifted to the ground. A second knock, and the door dragged open to reveal a women on the threshold.

'What?'

It was immediately apparent that this was the person I'd spoken to in the Electric – the one who'd told me Amade was too ill to receive visitors. Whether she recognised me was another matter. I introduced myself.

'I'm Larry Bridger. I um...I chanced across Mr Amade in town last night and he invited me round to talk about some work.'

An older woman loomed up beside this taciturn figure. If ever someone's personality was proclaimed by appearance it was so with the new arrival. Her woebegone features radiated a lifetime's accumulation of misery and mistrust. She leaned forward and murmured in her companion's ear, loud enough for me to hear.

'That's your husband's cape he's wearing.'

But now the first woman muttered 'I'll go and check with Martin,' and very soon afterwards Amade himself appeared in the doorway.

'Larry, isn't it? You found us then. Come in, come in.'

Amade took my elbow and guided me into his living room. 'You have just met my dear wife Connie,' he said. 'And...' – here he winked and dropped his voice to a conspiratorial whisper – 'My *mother-in-law*.' He gestured around the room. 'This is the nerve centre of my existence. We can get down to work here.'

I looked around to assimilate the details of Amade's working life. Neither he nor his wife had bothered to tidy the place up for their surprise visitor. Unwashed mugs and plates were dotted about the scanty second-hand furniture. A dish of half-eaten pasta perched on the arm of a ragamuffin sofa. Underfoot was a stained carpet of indefinite hue, in one corner of which detritus had piled up like driftwood on a sea shore – clothes, old newspapers, a pack of toilet rolls, a one-eyed teddy bear, a dusty violin. Elsewhere, books spilled from a bookcase made of planks mounted on bricks. It was clear that as a housewife 'Connie' subscribed to the old proverb 'Clean house, dull woman'.

Amade had followed my gaze and remarked 'I know what you're

thinking.'

'So, a clairvoyant!'

He laughed, not exactly the hyena cry, but still a sound like no other. 'It's all my fault, as Connie will tell you. We've changed houses so many times. I can't bear to be tied down.' He whirled in a circle, flapping his arms about. 'God, if only we had the money to travel. If only it was *possible* to travel, in safety I mean. Don't you love getting about, seeing the world?'

'I am *from* the world,' I told him. (**Ref 5**)

I was thinking something else too. I was thinking of my own crude room in Brum and the reason for its crudity – the same reason for Amade's threadbare surroundings. Poverty! His next comment suggested that he really could read people's minds.

'Ah Mr Bridger, if only the creative arts paid better, eh?' (**Ref 6**)

I said 'When I first came to this city I lived for months on bread and black olives. But tell me, do you think the lives we lead would be so different if we *were* properly remunerated – if our efforts were rewarded with an avalanche of gold coins? Wouldn't we do it anyway, whatever the outcome?'

He gripped my arm. 'I believe you are a man after my own heart.'

'But saying that, I'm sure you have made a fortune from the work I heard at the Electric last night.'

Again he squealed with laughter. 'Oh yes, I am as rich as Croesus now,' he cried, and crossed the room towards what was clearly his raison d'etre – an upright piano with musical scores piled extravagantly on top, not to mention several empty wine bottles. He virtually threw himself at the instrument and his hands raced across the keys generating a torrent of sound. I recognised a strand of melody from the previous evening's show. There was another noise, a thin quavering that I realised was Amade singing. It was immediately joined by a second voice as his wife entered the room warbling in a creditable alto. She stood beside her husband stroking his great mop of hair until they'd brought the duet to a charming conclusion.

Amade sprang up again. 'Well that's put the show to bed for good. Dearest, do you think you could bring our guest a mug of tea or coffee while we talk?'

She took my request and for the first time I sneaked a proper look at the lady. You wouldn't call her beautiful, but she possessed pitch black eyes which lent her features a striking individuality. And she had an unusually trim figure that was bound to attract male attention. She knew it too, as was clear from the way she left the room under my appreciative gaze. At that moment I felt in my bones that Mrs Amade and I would one day have other fish to fry. I do hope I'm right in this conjecture.

Amade clapped his hands. 'So Mr Bridger, you are a writer.'

'To be perfectly honest, I always regarded myself as a poet. That was my first love. But where making money is concerned, poets are ranked with railway porters and grave-diggers. Then I discovered a facility for stage writing, and modesty aside I've had my successes here. I've studied drama of every sort and have conceived a great passion for it.'

'Then we may make a match, for my own reading tends towards history and philosophy.'

'I've not written for a musical event,' I admitted, 'But hearing your work for the first time I wanted very much to do so.'

'I like your enthusiasm,' Amade cried. 'Tell me, what sort of qualities do you think a piece of serious musical theatre should aspire to?'

This obliged me to bullshit, which people say is one of my strengths. 'Plenty of action, movement around the stage,' I drawled, marshalling my thoughts. 'A lot of incident, by which I mean *variety* of incident. Striking characters, it goes without saying. And of course comedy...'

'Comedy! In *serious* musical theatre?'

'Certainly comedy. That is essential. Comedy springing from serious foundations, when it is most effective.'

'I am intrigued.'

After the wife returned with drinks, I tried to observe Amade more closely. He was unlike the man I'd expected. There was an unusual quality to his conversation – a childlike openness that might not always work to his advantage. Someone like me is always shooting a line, but with Amade what you saw was what you got. I trusted him already, though he couldn't entirely trust me. I felt he even sensed that too, which really spooked me out.

Now he got down to business. 'You mentioned a book you knew – a novel to use as plot.'

'Yes, I have an idea. No point in racking our brains if we can borrow from somebody else.'

'My sentiments too. If it was good enough for Shakespeare it's good enough for me.'

'There's a novelist called Alan Warner. Scottish. Started writing around the 1990s. Uneven output but always interesting. Often outrageous.'

'I don't know the name.'

'There's not many who do nowadays. It's just my weird taste. One of his early novels was called *The sopranos*. It's about teenage girls who visit Edinburgh for a singing competition with their school choir.' **(Ref 7)**

'I like writing for women's voices.'

'So much the better. The emphasis is on these five girls – their characters, what they want from life, the high jinks they get up to. I think I could fashion a good libretto from it.'

Amade raised one hand aloft. 'OK, give me one character from this book. See if I can come up with something. A few chords, maybe a theme.'

I stared at him. 'What, just like that?'

He shrugged. 'I'll have a go, eh? It can't hurt.'

'Well...all right, if you're sure. My favourite character is called Orla. A young girl, like the others, but she's ill. She has cancer and it doesn't look good. She's afraid she'll die without ever having sex. There's one completely disgraceful scene...I don't know if we could do that on stage...'

'We'll do it,' Amade cried.

'The thing about her is she's so spirited, despite everything. Bags of courage...'

Again he held up a hand to stop me, a sombre expression on his face. Then another of his headlong dives for the piano, as if he needed its embrace to live and breathe. He hung fire for a moment, hands over the keys, then began to play.

This was my first proper encounter with Amade's virtuosity and I stood on his mangy carpet staring in astonishment. What came out was a theme of such plangent originality and beauty that I at once knew this must be something he'd used before, something composed in a period of solitude and unflagging industry. It conveyed all the wistful tragedy of a young woman confronting pain and oblivion, but underpinned it with a perky second subject that proclaimed 'never mind darling, there's always hope, and I'm young, and what fun it will be along the way'. At the end Amade drew a notebook from his pocket and scribbled something inside, before swivelling round on the piano stool.

'What do you think?'

I was flabbergasted and I said so. 'But look,' I countered, that was a piece you composed in the past, wasn't it? It's wonderful, but would you be able to, I mean would you be *allowed* to use it again?'

'Larry, I wrote it a moment ago,' he said. 'It's new. That could be your Orla – if you like her.'

'*Like* her?' I'd run out of words, which was unusual for me. 'My dear Amade, you're...what I mean is, meeting you like this, I feel so excited. It's a new experience for me. It's extraordinary.' I looked again at this unprepossessing little man seated at his piano. It was the moment even I, a musical ignoramus, glimpsed what he might be able to do.

'It is rather good, isn't it.' He leapt to his feet laughing, the comedian after the tragedian. 'So, Mr fully-dressed Bridger...shall we have a go at it? Shall you and I work together? What do you think? I have other commitments but I can fit this into my schedule once you give me something written down.'

'You mean some sort of contract?'

'No, no, no – I mean an outline of the plot. And a few early scenes to get my teeth into.'

'Of course. I see. I'll get down to work straight away.'

There it was again. He'd immediately come clean about his other commitments. My own obligations were no doubt as heavy, probably more so, but what did *I* do? Kept it to myself. I can't help it.

The meeting with this extraordinary musician had gone better than I could've hoped, so I thought it wise to leave before the man changed his mind. But Amade had more.

'There's something else if we're to get this thing off the ground. Have you come across a lady called Sharon Adair?'

I said the name sounded familiar, and even that was untrue.

'A talented newcomer on the scene. But the thing is, she's got an auditorium at her disposal. We could do with that.'

'Blimey!' The word was out before I could stop myself. 'Aren't we getting a bit ahead of ourselves?'

'Come, Mr Bridger,' Amade teased. 'Not getting cold feet already?'

'Of course not.'

'Then I'll set up a meeting. I'll be in touch.'

We exchanged phone details, and again I prepared to leave. But now there was movement at Amade's front door as another visitor arrived. The newcomer and Mrs A were exchanging pleasantries in the hall.

Amade, head raised, was all attentiveness, like a bloodhound sniffing the air.

'My student.'

'I see. Do you have many?'

'No. Connie's always on about it because we need the money. But it goes utterly against my genius. Still, this girl...you'll see, she's different.'

The door opened and Mrs Amade ushered in a young woman. The composer took her hand, then looked as if an electric current had passed through his body. I saw the girl's lovely face and thought I understood.

'Meet Nancy Stourage,' he told me. And 'Nancy my dear, this is Larry Bridger. Good news. Mr Bridger and I may have a part for you. How would you like to play a teenage schoolgirl wasting away to an early grave?'

On the instant she began to play the part, giving a little mew of distress and mutating from a healthy youngster to someone mortally ill – the kind of physical illusion only the best actors can handle. I could have sworn the colour drained from her features. Just as quickly she relented to bestow a dazzling smile upon Amade.

'I've always wanted to die gracefully.'

Amade bid goodbye to me, and shepherded the girl towards the piano. His wife nodded in my direction to signify it was her job to see me off the premises. I fell in behind her but my head was full of Nancy Stourage – her beauty and self-possessed demeanour and the way Amade was so clearly in thrall to her. I wondered how Mrs A felt about this and raised an eyebrow as Stourage reached the piano with Amade's arm round her waist.

'Now don't you get excited, Mr Bridger,' murmured Mrs Amade once we were alone in the hallway. 'It's not the sort of attraction a man like you would understand.'

'A man like me, Mrs Amade. What *do* you mean?'

'Of course Martin's in love with her,' she went on. 'It's music – that's the sacred bond between them. I can't compete and I don't try. Don't trouble yourself to understand?'

What I thought I understood was that she was saying 'Theirs is a bond which mere mortals like you and me cannot aspire to'. Hey, it was an intimate moment of sorts between us and I was emboldened to make my move. It helped that her forearm, by accident or design, had brushed against mine.

I turned to face her. 'I've been meaning to ask whether it would be a good idea for me to have your phone details. I can see you are your husband's constant help and companion. I mean, supposing I can't make contact with the man himself...'

She gave a knowing look that was like an X-ray of my soul. 'I would expect nothing less of you, Mr Bridger.'

She had the front door open but at that moment the piano struck up, and Mrs A raised a peremptory hand. Then it came – a soprano voice of unbearable sweetness drifting through the dusty hallway, a siren sound that could lure countless sailors to destruction on the rocks. The hairs on the back of my neck stood up.

Mrs A gave vent to an involuntary sigh. 'The Countess,' she murmured obscurely. At which point she pointed to the door, and I stepped out into the street.

'Now give me your phone,' she demanded.

I complied. She keyed in a number before shoving the phone back in my hand and slamming the door. I got one glance from those disturbing black eyes before she disappeared from sight.

Outside, the burning heat of the day had faded. As I walked away down the street, Stourage's voice streamed from an open window. Shadowy buildings loomed up from the darkness.

References

(Ref 5) 'I am _from_ the world.' A reference to Bridger's Italian origins, and his previous domicile in Germany.

(Ref 6) Amade's money problems were acute at this time. The many begging letters to friends came to light after his death.

(Ref 7) 'The sopranos', by the Scottish novelist Alan Warner, was published in 1998. Bridger seemed unaware that a musical version of the book was performed at the Edinburgh Fringe in 2015, written by

Vicky Featherstone and Martin Love, directed by Lea Hall. One critic observed that it was 'more like a gig than a musical'.

March 27, 2035

Amade buzzed me a couple of days later about getting together. His suggested meeting place – St James Catholic church! I went along with it, though I'd not been in a church for years.

I arrived on time but he didn't. Only a handful of people were in the place. I eased myself into a pew near the back and at once remembered how diabolically uncomfortable these contraptions were, designed to mortify the flesh. As in all such institutions the building was a complete turn-off – cold, angular, the same dreary design as every other church in Christendom.

My spirits dive-bombed. I needed diversion, and a possible option was sitting in the same pew: a woman in her late thirties sporting a dress – an unusual item of clothing these days and more than handy, as things turned out. Nothing venture, I thought, and slid along the pew to have a word.

'Do you come here often?'

She raised a baleful eyebrow. 'Every month.'

'As regular as that! It's years since I've been in a church.'

'That doesn't surprise me.' She looked me me up and down. 'I'm waiting for confession, if you must know.' She nodded towards a wooden box contraption in the side aisle. 'Whoever's in there now is taking for ever.'

'So do you have a lot to confess then?'

'Bloody cheek!' she said, but didn't seem that bothered. 'Just the usual things. Not as much as you, I imagine.'

This was going swimmingly, and I moved to brush the back of my hand against her leg. 'Look, suppose you had a bit more to tell the priest chappie?'

And there you have it. Bingo! It's all about saying the right thing at the right time. She caught on straight away, and a minute later my hand was under that dress finding a rich reward. Before long her own fingers were wandering too, and now the forbidding surroundings afforded an extra frisson of pleasure. My companion pierced the holy silence with an audible gasp of pleasure, and I had to give her a little shush. I looked longingly towards the confession box and its promise of privacy, but a priest would be in residence and three's a crowd. A seed was planted for the future though.

The lady had already managed one epiphany and I was on the way to mine when a small figure with ebullient hair emerged from the booth. Amade. My new friend, anxious not to lose her place in a non-existent queue, high-tailed it over there. She threw a comment over her shoulder.

'It was a pleasure.'

'It almost was for me,' I told her retreating back. *Flagrante delicto* again; it was beginning to define my social life.

Amade saw me and scurried across. I was ready to leave, but he slumped down in the pew.

'Give me a moment.'

He was there for a while, head in hands. I could see sweat pouring down his face, and sat down to wait. It was a relief when he straightened up again, though his pallid countenance didn't inspire confidence.

'I dread the idea of illness,' he said shakily. 'Leaving Connie without support in these awful times...'

'Does this sort of thing happen often?'

'Now and then.' Amade drew a voluminous handkerchief from a pocket and mopped his brow. 'I was often ill when young. Jaundice, bronchitis, scarlet fever. They left their mark.'

'Shall I take you home?'

He shook his head. 'It passes. If we could just sit quietly for a while.'

'Of course.'

We sat in silence. The muffled church sounds, so long foreign to me, fell upon our ears. I fancied we could hear the murmuring priest-voice emanating from the confession booth. A whiff of incense lingered in the air. Near the altar, an old woman was lighting candles.

Amade was visibly reviving and I risked a comment. 'I'm astonished these places still exist.'

'The Catholic church will last till doomsday,' he intoned. 'It has endured so much.'

'Have you always believed?'

'Since I've been capable of conscious thought.'

For myself I could put little trust in such credulous, submissive doctrines during our darkest of dark ages, but not wishing to offend my new partner I kept these thoughts to myself. Without warning Amade rose from the pew, apparently recovered, and signalled that we were leaving.

'I'm all right now,' he said, and proceeded to lead me in an almost sprightly fashion through unfamiliar streets. Nobody paid any attention as we negotiated a complex network of desiccated buildings. I spotted the word 'PALACE' above a set of double doors. Amade pushed and in we went. The rows of seats that met my eyes proclaimed 'a theatre'.

As we entered, someone rose from a seat near the back; a woman in her mid-forties, dressed in black.

'Sharon Adair,' said Amade as he introduced us.

I shook the lady's hand. 'I'm astonished. I'm supposed to know about theatre and I'd no idea this place existed.'

'It's our little secret,' she admitted. 'Have you never heard of the Custard Factory?'

'*Custard*!'

She grinned. 'I know. Let's not go there. Many years ago this whole complex belonged to them. It included a 220-seat theatre which at some stage was upped to 350. I absolutely love having access to it.' (**Ref 8**)

'Sharon's come down here from the north,' said Amade.

'Leeds,' she confirmed. 'Not much happening there. This theatre was one of the reasons I moved.'

'Wait till you see her in action,' Amade went on. 'Sharon was sent to earth to rehearse actors and singers.'

She pulled a wry face. 'Yet I'm still rehearsing for my own life.'

Amade relayed for Sharon Adair the outline I'd given him of *The sopranos*. 'Libretto by Larry here, music by me,' he finished up. 'Do you think such a work might interest you?'

'If *you're* writing the music, I'll do it.' She turned to me. 'Forgive me, Larry – I'm sure your stuff is top class, but this guy's the one I already know about.'

'It's fine,' I told her. 'I had exactly the same reaction to him.'

'So what sort of date would we be looking at?' Amade asked.

Sharon Adair gave a thoughtful nod and named a time five months in the future. *Five months!* I waited for Amade to explode or break into mocking laughter, but he too nodded thoughtfully and said 'Let's do it'.

Five months. I'd got myself mixed up with a pair of nodding lunatics. I looked from one to the other but they were both perfectly serious.

'We'll write it as we go along,' said Amade.

'Ditto rehearse it,' said she. 'How many parts?'

Amade looked enquiringly in my direction. My brain was racing like a runaway locomotive. 'Well...six main parts – the sopranos. Convent schoolgirls.' I spoke deliberately, determined not to say 'er' or 'um' and reveal that I was planning on the hoof. 'Two adult nuns. Can we have a dozen more schoolgirls – a chorus, maybe?'

'Certainly.'

'And – I'll have to think – a handful of men. Different ages, doubling up on parts. Maybe singing, maybe not.'

She was nodding again. 'I tell you what we'll do. Years ago there was an outfit called Birmingham Opera. You'll know of it, Martin.'

'I've heard the name,' said Amade.

'It folded. Usual reasons – funding problems, declining interest. Anyway, their system was to use professional singers for the big roles alongside amateur singers and actors from the local community. I'm going to follow suit. May even revive the Birmingham Opera name.' **(Ref 9)**

'What sort of material did they do?' I asked.

'You name it. Went right through the standard repertoire, plus lots of new stuff. They were big news. And they performed in unconventional locations. School halls, semi-abandoned theatres. Weird places like redundant factories. They did 'Turn of the screw' in a disused condom factory. Of course it's different for me. I've got this place on tap.'

''I have another question,' Amade told her.

'I've been expecting it.'

'Instrumentalists. How many will this place fit in?'

'It's more a question of what we can afford. Those buggers are expensive.'

'Twenty,' said Amade.

'Out of the question. Ten.'

'No way. Fifteen.'

'A dozen. And don't say another word.'

'You strike a hard bargain,' Amade said, but he looked satisfied.

'Where we're going to find them is another story,' Adair went on. And to me 'I expect you're aware of this problem?'

I shuffled my feet. 'Actually, I'm not so well up on the music scene.'

'No! Fifteen years ago the UK had several large orchestras. We're talking big – fifty, sixty players. All gone. Fell away like the big band scene after World War 2.'

'What happened?' I asked, though I half knew the answer.

'Audiences died out, literally. Around year 2020 most concert-goers were in their sixties. Seventies. *Eighties*. People used to conk out in the stalls. Younger generations turned away from anything that took more than three minutes to play. So no audiences, no orchestras. There are still people who play, of course, but they're hard to find. And the quality's lower. Martin knows all this better than me.'

'I must have a cor anglais player,' Amade burst out.

Adair snorted. 'Good luck with that. You'll need to dig him up first.'

'There has to be somebody.' Amade turned to me. 'Let's track one down. Scour the city. Will you help?'

'A quest,' I said, though my heart sank.

'That's the spirit. Good man.'

The other two seemed perfectly at ease, as if all this high-tempo bartering came naturally to them, but I was frantic with worry. I've never minded hard work and I'm a quick operator, but there are only 24 hours in a day. After this loony conversation I couldn't imagine what shape my days were about to take. I longed to apply the brakes but shrank from revealing – before these consummate professionals – my own status as a professional chancer. I wanted to slip away before they committed me to anything else.

'So is that it?' I said meekly. 'Anything else I ought to know about?'

'Of course there's the cat,' Adair said.

'God, yes!' exclaimed Amade. 'Miaow, miaow.'

'The cat!'

'I should perhaps prepare you.' She was smirking. 'The stage manager has a cat. It lives here. It's, um...a bit unpredictable.'

'I don't get it.'

'It sometimes treads the boards during performances.'

'Oh! You mean it comes on stage? That's no good. Can't you get rid of the thing?'

'Ah but then I wouldn't have a stage manager.'

There was a lull in the conversation and I took the chance to look around the half-lit theatre.   To an unbeliever, the rows of empty seats and the curtained-off stage would have carried no significance. To a drama buff the place brimmed with the promise of future productions – spotlights and footlights, greasepaint, the expectant chatter of audiences. What would be the outcome of our endeavours here? I had no feel for the situation. Not for the first time, Amade seemed to anticipate my thoughts.

'I have a question.' He had his serious face on. 'More like a statement really. You know all too well the sort of world we live in. The way popular culture bumps along in the gutter. The unremitting tone of abuse, the endless recycling of tawdry images, of facile self-promotion, until we disappear up our own arses. Not to mention our tenuous grasp of existence itself on this dying planet. I ask you, Sharon – music, drama – these wonderful things we're contemplating – do they have a place in this bastard world?'

'But you know the answer already, Martin.' She spoke with utter composure, and I glimpsed the strength in this woman. 'Now is when they matter most of all. We simply must go on. Let's knock-em dead.'

References

(Ref 8) The Custard Factory. A complex of independent shops, cafés and bars were built on the site of what was once Bird's Custard Factory, in Birmingham's Cobb Street. They included a small theatre, which as Sharon Adair correctly stated, started off as a 220-seater.

(Ref 9) An organisation called the Birmingham Touring Opera was

formed in 1987 under the direction of Graham Vick. In 2001 the name
changed to Birmingham Opera. A feature of their productions was that
singers moved about amongst members of the audience, bringing a
sense of immediacy to the performances.

April 7, 2035

At Amade's place for our first 'creative' session, following the meeting
with Sharon Adair. Connie not about, though her taut, erotic
personality lurked in every crevice of the house. Amade plonked
himself at the piano, gave a brief rendering of his Orla theme, then
sprang up again.

'How are we going to do this?'

Collaboration is a tricky business, never more so than at its outset.
Could Amade and I turn out good work? Could we even get on
together? Who would do what, and when? Who would pace up and
down while his partner made notes (which was how it was always
depicted in books and films)? Everything was up for grabs.

'It's not easy, is it?' he said, with his uncanny knack of divining my
thoughts. 'Do you have some underlying approach for the work?'

'So many things. What about you?'

'I suppose one of them is – whatever the situation, however draconian
the action on stage, music must never offend the ear.'

'I see.' I thought carefully. 'I suppose one of mine is – always avoid
anti-climax, unless it's part of the plot.'

'Give me an example.'

'Picture two men in a Paris theatre, eighteenth century. A beautiful actress comes on stage. "My God, look at that," says the first man. "I must have that woman." "Be careful," warns his friend. "Already three men have died because of her." "Three men! But how?" His friend says "The first man was killed in a duel. The second jumped from the gallery of this very theatre." "And what about the third man?" "Well the third man was underneath the gallery when the second man jumped..."'

Amade gave one of his hyena cackles. 'I like that. I think we're going to get on, Larry. Now look, the first thing we must do is put together one really good scene. Something powerful and thought-provoking, to grab Sharon's attention and get her comprehensively on board.'

'I thought she *was* on board.'

'Oh she's 100% reliable, don't worry about that. Once Sharon agrees to something, she delivers. But if we can fire her up...well, so much the better.'

I sent my brain rummaging through the plot of The sopranos. 'I'm not sure,' I told him. 'So many possibilities.'

'What about...you said one scene was so outrageous it couldn't be done on stage. What about that one?'

Again Amade surprised me. For a man who sometimes seemed a sandwich short of a picnic he had a way of fastening onto the important things, putting them into context.

'All right then,' I told him. 'See what you think.'

I outlined the scene in question. The 16-year old Orla – one of the five 'sopranos' in the choir – is ill with cancer, expected to die. She's having radiotherapy, has lost two stone and all her hair. She languishes in hospital, visited by the other sopranos. Orla is obsessed with the notion that she's going to die before having experienced sex with a man. The ward next to Orla's has just one bed, in it a Scandinavian sailor covered in tattoos, dying of pancreatic cancer. He lies there unconscious, muttering to himself, morphine drips attached to his arms. Nobody has ever visited him. Orla, reeling from the hospital drugs, resolves to have sex with him.

My account was interrupted by Amade, leaping from the piano stand to bound across the room and back again.

'Yes, yes, yes. I love it.'

'I haven't finished yet.'

He ran to the piano and hammered out thunderous bass chords, at the same time wailing a discordant melody in a thin, falsetto voice; thence to a jumble of stuff in one corner to snatch up a violin and play a lachrymose melody. Habitually a quiet, unobtrusive figure, he now vibrated with energy. His pallid skin seemed to glow.

'Sharon's going to love it,' he said, flinging the violin down.

'You don't think the scene is over the top?'

'It's musical theatre, Larry. We can do whatever we want. Isn't life wonderful!'

I finished describing the Orla scene while Amade bounced round the room like an excited child.

Later he quietened down, and we sat down to drink tea. I'd nipped out to use the toilet while he brewed up, and passed the open door of a room that contained a full-sized snooker table. It seemed like a pricey acquisition for a family that was near the breadline. On my return I risked mentioning it.

'Our one extravagance,' Amade said. 'Connie plays. She's very good actually. I spend hours in there. Me and the snooker balls and the green cloth. The movement and symmetry. The creative impulse. The peace it brings. I'm prone to fits of melancholy, Larry. I do some of my best work at the snooker table. Wrote the whole of my G minor mass there, much good did it do me. It's had a single performance.'

He promised to brief Sharon Adair about Orla's hospital scene and to get a date for a first rehearsal in the Custard Theatre.

'Then the three of us will be under way,' he said with a wink. 'I can hardly wait.'

April 28, 2035

The Custard Theatre lay in darkness. The curtains opened on a dimly lit stage. I was lolling in the front row of the stalls, the only incumbent of the 300 seats. Sharon Adair's tall, black-garbed figure stood motionless in the aisle. Amade was nowhere to be seen, but the murmur of piano music from somewhere backstage betrayed his presence.

This was the first proper rehearsal of The sopranos' production schedule. That it had some resemblance to a dress rehearsal rather than the inchoate mumblings of actors in everyday dress was down to Sharon. 'She does this sometimes,' Amade had said. 'Goes to town on one of the early scenes. It fires up the blood, gets everyone on board. You'll see.' I felt privileged to be present. I thought of Alan Warner, who wrote the original scene in the novel, and hoped he would have liked what transpired.

As my eyes adjusted, I made out the shape of a bed on stage, a man half propped up under the covers, arms attached either side to drips that led to six-foot stands. He was muttering non-stop in a guttural bass voice.

A shaft of light flooded the stage with a fierceness that jolted me upright. It indicated the opening of a door, and now the figure of Nancy Stourage – in the role of Orla – entered and advanced towards the bed.

And what a figure! She bore little resemblance to the lovely young woman I'd met in Amade's house. This Orla was completely bald, wore a shift that reached down to her knees, and tottered across stage on pathetically thin legs. In my years of racketing about Britain's theatres I'd not come across another actress who could suggest such radical changes to her physical form; the girl was a magician whose sorcery defied understanding.

Stourage approached the dying sailor and took one of his hands in hers. As he continued to mumble she leaned to kiss his forehead and sang a melody of ridiculous sweetness, supported by a tremulous piano.

> 'You're no alone in the world.
>
> _I'm_ with you.
>
> I'll be like you soon.
>
> I'm _with_ you.'

I'd have gladly taken more of this passage, but now the action changed. I'd been curious as to how Sharon Adair would tackle the bad-taste spectacle of a sick young woman wanting sex with a dying man, and now we saw. To say 'no holds barred' was almost an understatement. Stourage reached under the bedclothes and the movements of her arm left no doubt she was manipulating the sailor's cock. Then she changed her approach, pulled back the bedclothes and in a swift movement straddled the sailor's recumbent body, sighing as she rubbed herself against him. Her sung words became harshly urgent.

> 'No, you need to be hard.

Be hard for me, hard for me.'

She changed tack again and thrust her head under the bedclothes to give the unconscious sailor fellatio. I reflected on my first meeting with Nancy Stourage in Amade's house – on the goody-goody sweetness of an unassuming young woman – and marvelled at the way she'd applied herself to this scene. In her hands, in Amade's and Sharon Adair's, it had become an episode seething with regret and longing, and I felt sure we'd been right to do it.

Of course *I* knew what was about to happen but the next sequence still set my pulse racing, for the sailor abruptly sat straight up in bed shouting and waving his arms about, while Amade sent out great booming chords on the piano and Stourage screamed and back-pedalled away from him. I fancied that an exclamation came from Sharon Adair on my left. Now the sailor slid both legs from the bed and came forward in a crazy, robotic walk, while his right arm pulled free of its drip and his left dragged its drip stand crashing to the ground. The sailor bellowed in sightless panic and Stourage gave vent to swooping shrieks of alarm. Amade went insane at the keyboard. I couldn't envisage what effect the scene would have upon an audience but my own response veered between hilarity and shock. Finally Stourage threw herself at the sailor's knees crying 'Sorry, sorry, sorry,' and a woman in a night sister's uniform entered stage right to give a cry of alarm. Sharon Adair called 'Cut'. The theatre lights came on and Amade rushed on stage clapping his hands.

Adair showered congratulations upon all and sundry and I applauded her. 'Of course on the night there'll be blood all over the place', she said.

May 4, 2035

An awkward conversation with Amade this morning, when he buzzed as I was drinking my first coffee of the day. He wanted me to accompany him to Suffolk the following week, to work with a small group devising a piece for the Snape Maltings International Festival. I told him I couldn't.

'I know it's short notice,' he said. 'The thing is, I absolutely love what we've done so far on *The sopranos*. I have a really good feeling about our association. Can you stretch a point and come with me?'

I'd discovered enough about Amade to know he was completely sincere – it was his worst fault – but I had to decline. Travelling is tiresome and dangerous these days, but that wasn't it. Quite simply, I had a work pile-up of epic proportions – something I should have (but hadn't) already confessed to Amade. I really had to be more disciplined about making and keeping commitments.

He took my refusal gracefully. 'Don't let it come between us, Larry. We're going to be great together.' And I could honestly say that I felt the same.

May 5, 2035

My embarrassment about refusing Amade's request to travel was partly down to an assignation I had with his wife the following day. The location for this, as things turned out, was to be the same St James church where I'd met Amade himself. Mrs A had refused to visit my 'miserable bedsit' (her words) and I was reluctant to squander hard-earned cash on some tacky motel. And besides, my hunch was that she'd be titillated by the improbable meeting place.

I arrived first and sat in one of the rear pews, having first peered into the confession booth and found it empty. As before the building was all but deserted, save for a couple of old crones prostrated before the altar. The church organ was groaning away in the background.

Mrs A arrived ten minutes late and stood in the aisle eyeing me with her customary hostility.

'I'm so pleased you came,' I told her.

'I had nothing else to do.'

A promising start. I jumped up and led her toward the confession booth.

'Where are you taking me?'

'You'll see. It's something different.'

I had a quick gander inside the booth before guiding her behind the curtain. She went without fuss. There was barely the space inside for two and she planted herself immovably in the middle of it. We pressed against each other willy nilly.

'Are you going to take my confession?' she murmured.

'God, no. That'd be a job and a half.'

'Just as well. I'm not into all that mumbo jumbo. That's Martin's side of things.'

'Nice to have this romantic organ music, isn't it?'

She fixed me with the gimlet eye. 'Look, I'm not interested in your tired old seduction routine, thanks very much.'

I tried a kiss, but she turned her head away. All the same, when I embraced the unyielding body and nuzzled her neck, the good lady did some heavy breathing despite herself; and when I slipped a hand down the front of her dress I found her body ready too. But then she took hold of my wrist and pulled me away.

'Of course, there's a price to pay,' she said.

'What!'

'You don't think you're getting this for nothing?'

For once I felt at loss with a woman. My hand fluttered towards a breast pocket but she bristled with scorn.

'How dare you!' Again the gimlet eye. 'Martin told me you wouldn't join him in Suffolk,' she hissed, so loudly that I pantomimed for her to lower the volume. 'Is that true?'

'Oh that! I've got too much work on. It's just not possible, believe me.'

'He needs you there.'

'I'd like to, but it's not on.'

She started to push me aside on her way out of the booth.

'No. Where are you going? Wait!'

She stopped. 'Well?'

'Bloody hell.' In recent weeks I'd had enough half-arsed sexual encounters to last a lifetime, and I didn't want more. She knew very well what I was feeling. She knew because she was like me. 'All right,' I said.

'You'll come to Suffolk with us?'

'Yes. Yes, all right, damn it.'

'And don't even think of changing your mind.'

What followed, though brief, was just what the doctor ordered. She thought so too, though she'd never have admitted it. At the end she exploded with such force that the confession booth rocked around us.

Then it was all over and she started adjusting her clothing. I'd collapsed, breathing heavily, onto the little seat they give you in these places.

She patted me briskly on the shoulder. 'Do your flies up before leaving, why don't you,' was her parting shot, and then there was nothing to indicate what had occurred but the earthy tang of her body and the little curtain swinging back and forth.

I sat distracted for a moment, pondering the mass of unfinished work I'd let myself in for, until a whisper of sound, halfway between a sigh and a groan, suggested that someone else had shown up. Alarmed, I leaned forward to peer through the mesh partition of the confessional. Above the clerical collar a face of singular antiquity palpitated in the darkness, and a voice croaked its ancient formula.

'Can I help you, my son?'

I was too disorientated to find the orthodox response. 'Oh, no, it's...er, it's fine sir...um father. I mean, I'm sorry, I just sat down here for a rest. I've not done anything that would interest you.'

'Just as you wish,' came the voice.

I left at the double and made for the exit. Out on the street a passer-by gestured towards my flies, which were gaping open.

May 12, 2035

Of course I cursed bitterly when the time arrived for going to Suffolk. Like most people these days I travel as little as possible. And when it means shelving a mountain of profitable work...well, that's hard to bear.

I met up with Amade and his missus at Birmingham's New Street station. It was my first visit there for two years and nothing had improved. The place was filthy with dirt and piled-up garbage. Areas that had formerly contained shops and cafés were taken over by homeless people, whose grimy mattresses littered the floor. In the main concourse, the station's automated display boards had long since fallen into disuse. New Street had a history of last-minute platform changes, but now there was little sign at all of integrated scheduling. The escalators weren't working, so passengers loitered in droves near the stairways and pounded down them when an official shouted out train arrivals. Disabled passengers didn't stand an earthly.

The itinerary to the festival was complicated. What we wanted was the coastal town of Aldeburgh, but it wasn't served by rail. Nearest thing was a small place called Saxmundham, where the festival people would catch up with us. Oh, and we had to change at Peterborough. I uttered some more choice expletives and wished I'd booted Mrs A. from the confession booth before she lured me into this wild goose chase.

The condition of the rolling stock was deplorable but we found three seats at the end of one coach. I ran a wary eye over the other passengers. Train travel was known for its rough-houses. If push came to shove I had a firearm in my pocket and would have used it too. However we were left alone. None of our fellow-travellers noticed that a top-rank composer was in their midst. Amade wasn't the sort to exude the airs and graces of celebrity. He knew his worth all right, but his outward demeanour gave nothing away. With his short stature and unexceptional features no-one gave him a second glance.

Maybe I should have felt a bit uneasy, sitting with the man I'd cuckolded and the woman I'd done it with, but that didn't seem to matter now. Mrs A. kindly produced some food for all three of us, and our conversation would have sounded perfectly natural to outsiders.

I asked Amade something I'd been pondering for the past few days. 'Tell me, why are you so keen to go to this festival?'

'They've always been good to me,' he said.

'Money,' his wife broke in. 'They pay well and we need the cash. And they *have* been good to Martin, it's true. He's always at his happiest there. Though how much things will have changed...I don't know.'

'What do you mean?' I asked.

'Let's wait and see.' She was looking evasive. 'They haven't told us much. It's so difficult finding out stuff nowadays.'

'And there's something else,' Amade said. 'Hagen will be at the Maltings. He's coming across from Germany.'

'Who?'

'Joseph Hagen? You've heard of him, surely?'

'I don't think so.'

'Come on, Larry. Hagen's *the* man. More highly regarded than any composer living.'

'Oh! Sor-*ree*.' Again I'd cast myself in the role of ignoramus. 'And you're in favour of this man?'

'Yes, he's OK. It makes a nice change, associating with someone of my own stature.'

I could never get used to this quirk in Amade's character. The most unassuming of men, he had an unshakable belief in his own genius where music was concerned.

'He often borrows stuff from my work,' Amade observed.

'Does he indeed! The little bugger.'

'No, no, no – that's not a problem. It's a kind of tribute. I borrow from him.'

'Hagen's a decent bloke,' Mrs A. piped up. 'A bit more grounded than my dear husband.'

Our train lumbered through a wasted English countryside. The colours depressed my spirits, especially when I remembered the bright fields of wheat and rape from childhood. Now so much was plain mud — that, and forests of unsightly weeds. Trails of rubbish lined the side of the track. On the fringes of towns came crumbling warehouses, junk-yards of abandoned vehicles, allotments running to seed. The roads were free of traffic save for the odd electric car — and of course the usual plethora of bicycles. We saw plenty of people living rough, in scraps of canvas laid out under trees or simply sprawled on ground-sheets. Outside one neighbourhood a raggle-taggle band of people had gathered around a bonfire formed from bits of furniture.

Amade's wife took a lively interest in her surroundings, but the composer himself barely looked out of the window. He was working, and clusters of notes flew from his fingers onto a manuscript that rested on our communal table. It would have taken an explosion to jog the man from his fog of concentration.

At Peterborough our train was delayed by an hour, and when we did get going it proceeded slowly. The region we were in now had a distinctly rustic flavour and the people who clambered aboard looked very different from Birmingham citizens. Mrs A raised an eyebrow but I don't think her husband noticed.

Around 5pm we reached Saxmundham, and everything changed. A young woman from the Maltings was waiting for our party and she and her driver took responsibility for everything. They transferred us to a smart vehicle and insisted on handling our luggage. I saw now why Amade had wanted to make the trip. These people were solicitous to his every need, and clearly delighted that he'd honoured them with his presence. A far cry from the take-it-or-leave-it treatment he got in Brum. Mrs A. and I garnered some reflected glory, and I made the most of it.

We passed quickly through Saxmundham, which was barely big enough to deserve a pillar box let alone a railway station, and moved past some Georgian houses and shop-fronts into open country. Our guide – Sarah – leaned round in the front passenger seat to address us.

'I don't know how much you're aware of what's happened round here. If you're interested, we could pass by the sea front first.'

Amade wasn't bothered, but his wife took up the offer. When we reached the place in question I almost regretted it. The car left the road to drive down a track formed from the recent movement of vehicle wheels across the land. We all alighted and Sarah gestured towards the 'sea-front', which was simply the point water had reached on that day. Mrs A was the first to look up, and gave a stifled cry.

'You see what I mean,' said Sarah.

In the surging water, at irregular intervals going out towards the horizon, were visible the upper parts of buildings that would have been residences and shops in the town of Aldeburgh. They sat there like indifferent references to a former age. You could only guess at what lay underneath the water. Half a town eaten alive by the encroaching ocean, a grotesque and unsettling sight.

'I had no idea,' I said.

Sarah shrugged. 'I'm not surprised. The government doesn't advertise stuff like this. But the sea keeps coming regardless, every week more so. It's all down the east coast. We get it bad because this is the most eastern settlement in the UK.' She moved back towards the vehicle. 'Come on, we'll show you something else.' (**Ref 10**)

Back in the car, we moved in a cautious semi-circle to conform to the unpredictable course of the water. The driver stopped by a row of houses where inundation was in its infancy, the water a mere couple of feet up the brickwork.

'Britten's house,' said Sarah. 'Where he and his lifelong companion use to live. 'It *was* a museum, but you can see we had to scrub that. OK, on we go.' (**Ref 11**)

A few minutes more and we'd reached our destination. We climbed out and stood gazing at another strange world. It had the random, accidental nature of certain Brum landscapes, but there the resemblance ended. A handful of unusual buildings were scattered about in various stages of decay, and heaps of sandbags lay everywhere. The essence of the place was flatness. The horizon stretched away for ever. A great expanse of rushes lay behind us, and water flowed past on one side.

'The river Waveney,' said Sarah. 'We have to keep an eye on that, as you can imagine.'

Above us, moody clouds drifted across a vast sky. Even Amade noticed it.

'The sky's so big,' he said, his first real observation since we left Brum.

References

(Ref 10) *From a 2060s standpoint, changes reported in the UK landscape at the time of Bridger's diary seem relatively modest. But the significant matter is that by the year 2036 a point of no return had been reached. Thanks to profligate governments burning up energy and individuals jet-setting around the globe and depredations of the rain forest, to wars in Asia and a confrontation between China and the west over Taiwan and all sorts of other problems, the polar ice caps had been damaged worse than anyone anticipated. Tides rose all round the world and the process was irreversible.*

(Ref 11) *The British composer Benjamin Britten and his lifelong partner, tenor Peter Pears, were the moving spirits behind the International*

Festival of the Arts launched from Aldeburgh in 1948. Snape Maltings, a few miles inland, was a cluster of buildings used until the 1960s for malting barley, after which they were adapted for musical events in accordance with Britten's ambitious vision for the area. However by the 2030s the festival, originally annual, was being held on a more irregular basis.

May 13, 2035

Soon after our arrival at Snape Maltings Sarah escorted Amade and myself to the office of the man in charge. (Mrs A. stayed behind to do her unpacking.) John Sumsion, Snape's director, occupied a makeshift office in one of the former malting buildings. He had a desk and a large photo of Benjamin Britten on the wall, and not much else. He greeted us warmly and thanked Sarah, who took her leave.

'I hope you've been well looked after,' Sumsion said.

Amade told him our reception had been all anyone could have wished.

'Sarah's a remarkable girl,' Sumsion went on. 'She's the most talented young flautist you'll ever hear, but she's thrown in her lot with us here at Snape. No task is too much trouble for her. She'd clean out the toilets if I asked her to. How much do you know about our operation?'

Amade said his knowledge was out of date.

'I never expected to be doing something like this,' Sumsion said, 'But now I wouldn't have it any other way. We provide a service for people who care. That's why I appreciate your coming here, Mr Amade. And you of course, Mr Bridger. The people who come here to listen, they may look like death warmed up – you'll see what I mean – but they cherish quality. They'd go to the ends of the earth to hear music by yourselves or Mr Hagen.'

He broke off as a young woman came in with coffee.

'Tell me about the Birmingham scene,' Sumsion resumed. 'I no longer have any feel for the rest of the country.'

Amade shook his head. 'Not good, I'm afraid. A few of us struggle on. It's hard to make a living.'

'And if *you* say that...tell me, what was your first impression, coming into this place from the outside?'

Amade grimaced, but struggled to reply.

'No, that's not fair of me. I'll answer my own question. It's like the end of the world. A last bastion for the real enthusiasts. A place where genuine quality is more important than appearances. That's why you've been asked here. Get down to work as soon as you can. And you must come to this evening's concert.'

After travelling all day the last thing I needed was work, but Amade never thought of much else. I showed willing and sat with him for an hour while Connie pottered in the background. We already knew our task, and had started on it in Brum. Apparently Britten's best-known opera was called *Peter Grimes*, about some rum cove in an east coast fishing village who was ostracised by most of the community, not least because he was thought to have killed a small boy. A strange subject for an opera, if you ask me. Our assignment was to take this character and this setting and fashion a modern alternative, echoing Britten's music along the way. A Britten tribute, in other words. By now I knew well enough that Amade was the right man to pay homage. He could do it standing on his head. He could come up with a pastiche of any musical style under the sun, from Wagner to Louis Armstrong to the black rappers who masquerade as musicians in nite-spots all over the capital.

We broke off from work as soon as I could wangle it and agreed to meet for a drink before the evening concert. It was in a place they called the Hoffman Building, which had a 340-seater auditorium – large enough, apparently, to satisfy demand in these troubled times. The various buildings on the site are relatively close to each other, and walking is the Snape custom. As Amade, Connie and I trudged across, the light was beginning to fail. There was a spitting of rain from the stifling climate that is so characteristic of these times. Connie wore a dress, which made her look younger and less forbidding – and heels, which gave her trouble on the rough ground.

As we approached the Hoffman an extraordinary spectacle met our eyes. To one side – away from the entrance, but still in full sight – were dozens of canvas tents. As I looked, an old man crawled from one of them, wearing a threadbare parody of smart-casual evening dress.

'So that's their accommodation,' Connie observed.

'Surely not!' I exclaimed.

'You want to bet? Poor buggers – they'll be getting hell from the mosquitoes.'

Confirmation of a kind came as we moved inside the building. A bar had been set up just inside the entrance and two blokes and a woman were serving drinks; the woman none other than Sarah, flautist, meeter-and-greeter, and now barmaid. But what you couldn't help noticing was the appearance of those being served. The bloke I'd seen crawling from his tent was representative. Around him were dozens of men and a few women from the same stable – average age surely no less than 75 and often a good deal older. Some, patently unable to stand, had subsided into chairs. Others were in wheelchairs. This motley crew wore all the unsightly insignia of age on their persons, let alone the red blotches that confirmed Connie's prophecy about mosquitoes (the monster blood-suckers we've become accustomed to nowadays). Touchingly, people had attempted to look smart for the occasion; jackets that had seen better days, some neck ties and even bow ties, party dresses on the women. To judge by the accents that rose above the communal din, most of the men had been to public schools. There was a sense of excitement in the air that seemed genuine rather than forced. I'd heard Amade talk about the geriatric concert audiences of the early 2020s, and these people were a remnant of even that era. They'd made their way to Snape Maltings from all over England because music was what they cared about; what they cherished, in Sumsion's term. They were the last of their breed. They were like the driftwood that accumulated on beaches after a heavy tide. Why their younger compatriots don't respond to serious music is beyond my capacity to say. I doubt whether Amade could answer either, though he continues to write such music himself for a largely non-existent audience. Perhaps the whole lot of them suffer from delusions. Perhaps they're the only sane people in a crumbling universe. I wouldn't know.

Amade and his missus were soon swallowed up by the oldsters, leaving me alone by the bar to nurse my drink. I didn't know a soul there except Sumsion and the flautist girl, yet now a man approached me.

'Mr Bridger?'

'Why yes.'

The newcomer extended a hand, and in the moment of shaking it I registered the German accent.

'I'm Joseph Hagen.' (**R 12**)

He was a lot taller than Amade – who wasn't? – and quite a bit older. Unlike Amade he looked composed, at peace with himself, especially standing amongst this collection of coffin-dodgers.

'I understand you're working with Martin on *Peter Grimes*?' Hagen said.

'We've made a start.' I was so ignorant about Hagen's work that it was hard to move the conversation on. 'Are you an admirer of Britten'?' I tried.

Hagen pursed his lips. 'He had many qualities. I find the concentration on male characters rather relentless, but still...amongst English composers...'

'Of which there haven't been that many,' I interrupted, and reflecting that even I could reel off a list of eminent Germans, added 'Unlike your own country.'

Hagen nodded. 'We've had a few. Maybe...'

'I'm sorry?' The din from the oldsters had risen to a crescendo and I only half caught his words. I reached out to guide the pair of us away from the throng. Behind me, Sarah was trying to support an old codger who'd collapsed across the bar. 'Such a scrum in here,' I said, from the relative peace of our new situation. 'This is the sort of scene St Peter must face outside the pearly gates.'

If Hagen was amused by this he didn't let on. 'I was saying that Purcell may have been the best of the English composers,' he observed. 'That is, until now.' And when I looked blank, 'I'm referring to *Martin*. Martin Amade, of course. He's the best of British. Come to that, the best of German too.'

I could see Amade still deep in conversation on the other side of the room. 'But Mr Hagen, Martin is an enormous admirer of your own work. He says you're more highly regarded than any living composer.'

'I do all right,' Hagen agreed. 'But I have to tell you, I cannot compare with Martin Amade.'

'Really!'

'I can assure you. Perhaps he is the greatest we've known. Of course, such matters are hard to determine, but Martin does things none of us can match. There is no recognition of this in your own country, but *I* know, and I expect Martin knows it too. I tell you, Mr Bridger, cherish this man. We will not see his like again.' That 'cherish' word again; the very expression Sumsion had used in his office.

The concert got under way a few minutes later. I had the impression the event was somewhat thrown together, but hey, it happened didn't it, and before a highly enthusiastic audience. One of the early items was a Hagen string quartet. The pensioners loved it but Mrs A, who was sitting next to me, leaned across to whisper that the viola player was weak. It all sounded much the same to me. Next up, and more to my taste, was a song called 'Lord Maxwell's goodnight', which had once been recorded by this Peter Pears chap, Britten's long-term squeeze. And after that, blow me, Amade himself jumped up from the audience and went on stage to perform a Hagen violin sonata. A nice tribute to his friend and the old-stagers went crazy, but Connie looked nervous. 'He's a bit rusty on the fiddle,' she whispered. 'He's had to choose one of the early sonatas because they're easier.'

After the interval came the big surprise. We'd just settled back into our seats when a gaggle of instrumentalists marched onto the stage, followed by Hagen with a mike in his hand. He made a short speech to the effect that his friend Martin Amade was a great man, etcetera, etcetera, and that to mark Amade's presence at Snape they were going to perform his renowned piece for 13 wind instruments. I heard a strangled exclamation from Amade on my left, and saw Connie reach out to put her hand over his. Then Hagen rapped on the conductor's lectern with a baton, and off they went. I could almost feel Amade's emotional response and when I stole a quick look, tears were coursing down his face.

Amongst the 13 players was Sarah, who'd changed out of her barmaid's clothes and played an electrifying passage on the flute. I thought of Sumsion's comment about her 'cleaning the toilets', and kept picturing the girl on her knees scrubbing a lavatory bowl.

At the end of the piece, 45 minutes later, Hagen beckoned Amade down to the stage and the two men linked arms to acknowledge a frenzied reception from the audience. Connie was discreetly wiping her eyes with a handkerchief. It was quite an occasion.

I'm writing this diary entry after breakfast on our second day at Snape. There was a sad corollary to yesterday's concert, because they've just pulled the body of an old man out of the Waveney. Seems he didn't return to his tent that evening but went straight down to the river. Speculation was that he'd been overwhelmed by the concert and decided to go out on a high. I probably caught a glimpse of him in the bar beforehand, poor old git.

Reference

(Ref 12) Joseph Hagen, a prolific Austrian composer, was (after Amade) the best-known musician of his time. He was 24 years older than Mozart and outlived him by a further 18 years, but the age difference was no barrier to their congenial relationship. Their meeting at Snape seems to have eluded the attention of historians.

May 15, 2035

Back in Brum, with mixed memories of Snape. It's a hard place to love but you have to admit they do the business. For how much longer though, with water lapping at the sandbags on their doorstep? I overheard one of the wrinklies refer to John Sumsion, the director, as 'King Canute'.

I left Suffolk before Amade, after four days of working as hard as I've worked in my life (but see below). I'd knocked the *Peter Grimes* libretto into shape, and can do more when Amade returns. His own work rate defies belief. Of course it's powered by his extraordinary talents, which I'm only now getting into focus. I'm a hard worker myself, and after five or six drafts can usually fabricate something that's half-decent, but Amade, hah! – he sits at the breakfast table, coffee in one hand and pen in the other, turning out deathless material at the first time of asking, damn his eyes. It takes it out of him though. Being a genius has a price attached. I told Connie about the first time I set eyes on her husband as he cavorted on a public highway pretending to be a dog. 'I don't see those high spirits now,' I said. Her response?: 'For god's sake, Larry, why do you think that is? He's not well – surely you can see that. He's not well and it weighs on his mind. He worries about leaving me with no means of support. I wish he wouldn't.'

I've had to revise my opinion of Connie. I used to think she was a flibbertigibbet, a millstone round her husband's neck, but she's more than that. She knows enough about the music side to be a sympathetic ear, which is more than most of us can manage. She cares about him, and he in turn is sustained by her warmth. She's all right. (**Ref 13**)

I'm writing this entry in my bedsit in a state of pleasurable exhaustion. Because of the unplanned sojourn in Snape I came back to a pile-up of overdue work that was doing my head in. Not that there's anything worthwhile about these assignments (hopefully apart from the stuff with Amade) but that's not the point. As a jobbing writer of no fixed employment, it's my experience that punctuality is just as important as quality – probably more so, since most of my clients wouldn't recognise quality if it jumped up and bit them on the bum. I've always been good at turning out prompt copy, even if it meant burning the midnight oil. Until now... So what happened yesterday was a miracle. I'm putting the seductive details in this diary, so I can wallow in their pleasures later.

I'll start at the beginning. My bedsit, first. It's a miserable hole in a bad part of town. Poorly furnished and the electrics are up the spout. I avoid taking women there unless they're such wanton slappers that their opinion of me doesn't matter.

The building is owned by a widowed dressmaker, an odd woman with a habit of running an imaginary tape measure over visiting strangers. She leaves tailors' dummies standing around in the entrance hall, which can be disturbing in a dim light. The best thing about this lady is a 16-year old daughter called Angelique, who I'd only spoken to once or twice before.

Yesterday I'd told the landlady I had to devote the entire day to work and couldn't be disturbed. *She* told *me* she'd be away for 24 hours and was leaving the daughter to handle any emergencies. Events did not turn out as I'd imagined. At 8am as I started work (*two hours* earlier than usual) there came a tap on my door. Angelique stood on the threshold with a flask of coffee.

'Is that for me?'

'My mother said I had to look after you.'

I took the flask. 'Angelique, this is very nice of you.'

She paused very deliberately before speaking again. 'I can do more.'

I took a second look. She wore a simple white shift that ended just above her knees, and the scent of her body penetrated the coffee fumes. 'This girl could be my grand-daughter,' I told myself. 'Get on with your work, Bridger.'

'Mum told me you're very busy,' she said, speaking slowly and clearly, like an even younger child. 'Tell me what it is you have to do.'

I told her there were four different assignments to complete, and I'd be working into the small hours. With the same placid composure, she said that she could help.

'Why would you do this?'

'I'm sixteen.'

'I see,' I said, not seeing at all.

'Would you like to try it?'

Well...this is what happened.

She said that my first task, if completed on time, would be rewarded with a lunch of freshly cooked pasta. This notion, so inimical to my bedsit way of life, proved an effective inducement. I was writing a script for a midnight cabaret that featured some seriously troubled artistes of indeterminate gender. I'd witnessed the show a fortnight earlier and persuaded the manager they needed some new sketches, which is what I wrote now: a robed figure with long blond hair enters with back to the audience and sings like Marlene Dietrich, then rips off the costume to reveal a grossly fat man swathed in bandages; two young women act out lewd scenes from their days at a convent school, then one of them nails the other to a cross; a woman coated in gold leaf washes off the paint, then pulls a gold balloon from her arse and inflates it; a creepy compère in a kilt dallies with a young girl in Nazi uniform and a dildo. Nothing special, but distinct improvements upon the original. I reckon the worst that could happen would be one of the show's audience making a citizen's arrest.

Around mid-day Angelique read the script, nodded gravely, and returned 20 minutes later with a dish of superior pasta. The girl ate with me in the room and revealed that she would stay there until the second task was completed. Normally I detest writing when someone else is in the room, but surprisingly Angelique's presence was no trouble at all. She sat silent in an upright chair with a stillness that confounded my notion of teenage girls. When I looked up she met my gaze with an unblinking stare from which I derived an unfathomable sensation of support. Occasionally I asked her opinion about the way women would behave in certain situations, and she gave lucid answers.

The show was one that I'd seen and liked, but which badly needed an injection of new one-liners and jokes. The performers were four men dressed as women, who sang and danced various exotic numbers. They looked and sounded like women and the producer insisted that they'd had the operation; they were certainly more confident in their sexual orientation than the performers of the cabaret.

When I'd finished, Angelique read the script and said she liked that one too.

'I don't believe this is happening,' I told her.

She urged me to continue with the third task. Often in the afternoons I'm assailed by waves of sleepiness that only strong coffee can counteract, but not on this occasion. I felt limber and unusually clear in the head, like a man who'd been hypnotised into cogency. Angelique left me now, saying she'd return in two or three hours when she hoped she could bestow a reward that would prepare me for the fourth and last task of the day. I have never in my life set to work with such vigour.

The third task, commissioned by a TV producer I know, was to write a play about an 18th century character called Charles Lamb. You don't turn producers down, but I was reluctant to take the gig because no-one I knew had heard of the guy. Of course once I discovered Lamb was famous for writing essays my enthusiasm knew no bounds! Turned out Lamb's grave is where my producer friend grew up – the north London suburb called Edmonton, now distinguished by drugs, turf wars, shootings, stabbings and every kind of mayhem. I'd already done the research for this project and now I quite enjoyed writing it. Lamb, who'd been friendly with the poets Coleridge and Wordsworth, was an interesting guy with a serious drink problem and a mad sister who stabbed their mother through the heart over dinner. I'm optimistic that my play will be shown on an unknown channel in the small hours, sandwiched between 15-minute bouts of advertising. I don't care as long as they pay me.

Now then. I summoned Angelique and she read through the first draft of the play and said it was the best thing I'd written all day. I refrained from enquiring about the promised reward, because the mind of a 16-year old girl is unknown territory and I knew only that she was in charge of matters.

I didn't have to wait long.

'Would you like to come over here, Mr Bridger,' she said.

I went and stood by where she was sitting. She looked up at me. 'I should like to kiss you, Mr Bridger, but my mother has insisted that I must never kiss older men.'

'That's a pity,' I said.

'Even so, that leaves some latitude.'

'I don't understand.'

She took my hand and placed it on the upper part of her white dress. In no time I was fondling the pneumatic breasts that jostled inside; I had not experienced their equal for many years. She sat imperturbably, staring into my eyes. I was tremendously aroused, and feeling that the little minx knew exactly what she was doing, I waited for her to speak again.

'You need not restrict yourself to my breasts,' she said, in the same even tone – like that of a student at an elocution lesson. So saying, she sat back in the chair and drew her legs apart.

I won't say what happened next, except to report that she wore nothing underneath the dress and that she began to breathe more deeply. I want to stress that over those few minutes I exercised more self-control than I have in my whole life.

My hand was still at work when she spoke again; I thought that her voice was quavering a little.

'Shall we move on to your fourth task, Mr Bridger?'

'I am in your hands.'

'Surely the other way around,' she said, rising to her feet. 'I am grateful for your forbearance. If you complete your fourth task there will be a similar experience, which I hope you would find pleasurable.'

The fourth task was to write another act of *The sopranos* for Amade. Already, hours of labour lay behind me that day, but thanks to the machinations of this virginal nymphet, I fizzed with manic energy.

When I'd completed the work, our coming together was marked with the same restraint that defined the girl, yet it will remain one of the most erotic experiences of my life. Afterwards she stood at my side, handkerchief in hand, and enquired sweetly 'Are you happy with me, Mr Bridger?'

I said I could give many different replies to her question, all of them positive.

'Of course you know we must not do this again.'

'It is as you wish.'

'I am grateful to you. Please think of me sometimes.'

'I shall do more than that,' I replied.

Reference

(Ref 13) Bridger's thoughts on Connie are a useful corrective to the views of Amade's biographers, who have generally given her a bad press. Of course we know from the diary that she was not entirely a faithful wife, but that is unlikely to have been a preoccupation for Amade at the tag end of his life. Her practical support would have been much more significant.

May 18, 2035

Another writing/composing session with Amade today for our collaboration on *The sopranos*. I have been looking back over the entries in this diary, and it strikes me they've been dominated by references to the composer. This was not my original intention, but something about the man seems to have got under my skin.

He makes an interesting psychological study. In times like these when our very survival is at stake, self-interest becomes the prevailing element of the human condition; god knows, I'm as bad as the rest. Amade though is a different case. He'll do anything to further his music, but that's about dedication to a cause rather than personal advancement. It is almost fair to say that his passion is for getting the music *composed*, rather than having it performed, the latter being so chancy these days. All very idealistic, but his attitude causes friction with Connie, who is in charge of their finances. The couple are poorer than church mice.

As to the quality of Amade's music, I am not the man to ask. Hagen was convinced, and he seems to be the cat's whiskers in their little world. What I have noticed is that as Amade's time gets shorter, or so Connie has hinted, his output is ever more concentrated. Everything he writes now – including when it's for works of a comic nature – contains passages of unearthly perfection that are apparent even to the likes of me. There is a sense of desperate haste about the man, a racing against time to unburden himself. Does that make sense? I wish I weren't so ignorant about these matters.

There's another things I've noticed, reflecting on the jobs I've been doing now and for all my adult life – those mongrel vehicles for dodgy impresarios, performed by superannuated actors in half-empty theatres – and that's a weird feeling that out of the whole caboodle it'll be these collaborations with Amade that stand the test of time; that thanks to

Amade, words I'm writing now will still be read when I'm dead and gone and the worms are squirming through what remains of my sorry carcass. Just a cheery thought for the day.

May 20, 2035

What kind of rubbish diary am I running here? I completely forgot to record a spooky incident that happened as the Amades and I were travelling to Suffolk. The three of us were at New Street station, hovering by the stairways waiting for our train to be announced, when a stranger came up and spoke to us.

'Mr Amade?'

'Why yes.' Amade looked puzzled. 'We've not met before, have we?'

Explanations were made. It seems the stranger had phoned Amade at home an hour before and been told about the Suffolk trip, so he'd taken a chance and intercepted his quarry at the station. The man was dressed from head to foot in the blackest of black clothes. This, and his manner – courteous enough but poker-faced – generated a slight sense of unease. He gave no name but said he would like to be known as Jacques.

'I am representing my master, who is a passionate fan of Mr Amade's music,' he announced. 'My master wishes to remain anonymous.'

'We don't do anonymous,' said Connie.

'Hear the man out, love,' Amade urged.

'So what's all this about?' Connie continued, always keen to cut to the chase.

Jacques gave a little bow. 'My master wishes to commission your husband to write an oratorio.'

'An oratorio, blimey,' said Connie.

'He has been very specific about the length, which he puts at 45 minutes.'

All three of us were leaning towards the man to pick up his words, which got lost amongst the tumult of anxious travellers. An official went past shouting a destination and dozens of passengers rushed the stairways, forming a bottleneck at the top.

'It's not our train,' Mrs A told her husband. And to Jacques, 'Now look, we really haven't got time for this. My husband's a very busy man. What kind of oratorio, anyway?'

'My master wants it to be on a theme of vampires.'

The stranger's words were half-lost in the hubbub, and Mrs A advanced upon him.

'Are you having a laugh? Did you say *vampires*?'

'That is correct, madam. We thought, a fresh angle.'

In the preceding 30 years the subject of vampires has been worn to death by all forms of the media. Every week brings a new vampire feature film that generally goes straight to streaming services, or whatever they're called nowadays. The most popular TV soap opera, *Your throat entices*, has been running for five years on the biggest commercial channel. Animated TV vampire films are the favourite genre for the under-threes.

'Please don't waste our time,' Mrs A told the stranger. I recognised her expression from the first time she'd opened the front door of her house to me.

In reply Jacques drew a bundle of bank notes from a jacket pocket.

Paper money has made a come-back since on-line services turned unreliable, but a bundle of this size is highly unusual. Mrs A executed a double-take before wonderingly taking hold of the notes and riffling through them, holding some up to the light. She sidled towards her husband and spoke from a corner of her mouth.

'Five hundred.'

Amade stared at her. 'So what do you think?'

Instantly she went off on one. 'And where the hell d'you think you'll find the time to write this...this...*vampire twaddle*?'

I saw what was going on here. She deplored the idea of Amade accepting this work, mostly on the (commendable) grounds of his failing health. As for Amade, he'd given no sign either way. If he were interested it would be in the work, not the money. Then again Connie wanted the dough but not the work. In effect she was arguing with herself. Women do it all the time.

She took possession of the banknotes in a manner that was casual, almost negligent. 'I'll sign a receipt if you make one out,' she said.

'No, no – that won't be necessary.' The stranger waved the notion away. 'Regard that as a down-payment. I shall be in touch again. About the work itself, there was...um...there was one suggestion that my master made.'

'I'm sure my husband can manage a simple oratorio,' Connie said.

'It was...in case of difficulty, go back to the source.'

'The source?'

'Mr Bram Stoker. His language.'

'I see.'

At this point a second official went past intoning the details of our train, and there was another rush for the steps.

The stranger raised his hat in an old-fashioned gesture. Amade shook his hand and Mrs A turned away to join the rush. Tucked inside her brassiere, next to the skin, was more money than she'd have seen in a long while.

June 7, 2035

A distressing composing session with Amade, though as a dramatist I couldn't help finding it interesting. Whatever projects we collaborate on in future – and I hope there'll be some – none of them can contain as much irony and pathos and dramatic content as Amade's own life.

His Suffolk tribute to *Peter Grimes* had clearly gone down well and he'd taken succour from it. Even a genius appreciates an occasional bouquet from his public. But his physical problems are harder to resolve, and I was shortly to get a striking demonstration of this.

Connie had met me at the front door with a litany of concerns. 'It's this fucking oratorio,' she murmured, using the f-word for the first time in my hearing. 'I mean...*vampire oratorio*...what the fuck is that when it's at home?'

'Is it just too much work for him?' I asked. 'Is that his problem?'

'It's more than that. The work' – she made a helpless little gesture – 'Whatever the work is, Martin gives it 110%. Always has done, always will. For him it's not work at all – it's like walking or breathing.'

'Well what then?'

'This vampire piffle. He's thrown himself into it like he does with everything, but...it's so *unhealthy*. Martin's creations...they're not joke vampires like you get in that ridiculous TV soap. His vampires are horrible creatures. You should hear some of the music he's done – if you can call it music. It frightens the living daylights out of me.'

'Do you wish you...he...hadn't accepted the commission?'

Connie didn't answer at first and I realised she was crying; silent tears that rolled down her screwed-up little face. That was one surprise. Another was, she took a step forward and clasped me against her.

'Don't go getting ideas,' she said.

I said I wouldn't and meant it. I was finding that I liked being her confidant. That brief coupling in the church confessional had taken our liaison in an unexpected direction. The mutual secret brought us closer, but constrained any further intimacy.

Her body convulsed, not unlike an orgasm. 'I don't know what to do,' she whimpered. 'I'm so lonely, you've no idea.' Unexpectedly she giggled. 'And you're no help, always pushing your bunch of teenage sexpots into his head. God help me, I don't know whether to laugh or cry.'

Amade called out from the lounge and we had to break up the confab. I went through and found him at the keyboard eyeing my fledgling script for *The sopranos*. He looked paler than usual but intent on the task ahead.

'This scene in the john,' he said. 'I've not got the feel of it yet. What kind of women are they?'

Connie had appeared and seemed to be settling in for the session, which was a new development. 'They're bad girls, Martin,' she said.

'They're teenage girls,' I said, Wild, immature, *real*. There's a pattern of behaviour at the convent school they belong to. Twenty seven schoolgirls from that place have got themselves pregnant in the preceding 12 months. Down in the town the school is known as the virgin mega-store.'

Connie laughed but Amade didn't.

'Got it,' he said, picking up a pencil from the side of the piano.

'So here's the background to this scene,' I went on. 'The entire choir of girls – along with the two nuns in charge – are travelling into Edinburgh by bus to take part in the semi-finals of a competition. *En route* they have a pit stop at an old hotel full of American tourists. The five 'sopranos', the clique of main characters, want to doll themselves up for the city. There's a queue at the 'Ladies' toilet, so they go into the 'Gents', and the action takes place there.

Amade threw himself into composing the scene with his usual vigour. Its frantic nature wasn't entirely suited to his gifts but he saw how such a sequence fitted into the plot. I was struck by the contrast between the quick-fire dramatic action and the quiet desperation of Amade's demeanour. He didn't hold back. His fingers flew across the manuscript paper scattering notes hither and thither. Creative aspects aside, it was a feat of physical dexterity. I'd once asked why he shunned the various IT programmes that were available to support composition.

'They don't suit my crazy methods of creating,' he'd replied. 'I like to feel notes cascading from my finger-tips. And to be honest, Larry – don't tell the PR people – we're always getting the electric shut off here because we don't pay our bills.'

We'd been working flat out for an hour or so when something happened that scared me stiff. Amade dropped his pencil and pitched headlong off the piano stall onto the carpet. I made a move towards him but Connie was quicker. She was down on her knees, turning his body over,

propping the head on cushions. As if an alarm had sounded, the mother-in-law emerged from nowhere to help; I'd not set eyes on *her* since my first ever visit to the house. Leaning over Amade's prostrate form, moving the limbs about, the two women might have been undertakers; the older woman's lugubrious features would have been suited to the role.

'Get me some water from the kitchen,' Connie demanded.

When I returned, Amade was still out cold.

'Has this happened before?' I asked.

'Oh yes.' She was splashing water on Amade's face. 'He gets carried away, and...wham, down he goes. If I could persuade him to give up composing, I would. But then I might as well take an axe to his head. All right, mum, thanks.' She dismissed her mother, who drifted from the room like a weary wraith.

'He told me about illnesses he had when younger,' I said.

'Oh yes? I bet he didn't come clean about that.'

'Oh, I think so...rheumatic fever and pneumonia.'

'And yellow jaundice, colic, nephritis, high blood pressure, bronchitis (every winter)...and kidney failure, of course, which often leads to blackouts.'

'I see.'

'What do I know,' she said. 'The life force must be there in spades or he'd be dead already. If you ask me, the illnesses are only part of it. It's his situation that's just as responsible for *this*...' She gestured towards the still immobile figure.

'What do you mean?'

'Martin's not suited to this world. He sees every bloody thing, the best and the worst, but he sees it like a child. And he's lonely up there on his pinnacle. No-one can help him.'

'You do.'

'I soothe his brow, wipe his arse for him. He needs the esteem of equals.'

'But surely...'

'They're afraid of him. It's his own fault. Never a good word to say for other composers. All right, so he's better than them, but he doesn't have to keep saying it.'

'Hagen though...'

'Hmm. Even there. He made a comment about Joseph Hagen in Suffolk. Something that was unfair and wrong. Of course it got back to the great man.'

'And what did Hagen do?'

'Nothing. He said "I forgive him". Hagen's a good guy.'

I'd not heard her speak so critically but it didn't really surprise me. And in a way, what did it matter? I looked at Amade, still prone and spread-eagled, Mrs A above him streaming with perspiration.

'Should I get a doctor?'

'Can't afford it. No, he'll come round – you'll see.' She looked up at me and, it seemed, right through me. 'Then one day he won't.'

Of course Connie knew what she was doing. These fainting fits were a frequent occurrence – only she knew how frequent. Eventually Amade groaned and rolled over and she helped him into an armchair and brought him brandy, the remedy for kick-starting his system. That wasn't the end of it. I was in the kitchen helping her to make strong coffee when we heard the sound of the piano. Connie clucked in frustration. Back in the lounge Amade was hunched over the keys like a man who'd risen from his deathbed. He was playing an adagio, a piece of such measured, ethereal beauty that irritation with its creator would have been an irrelevance. Connie crossed the room to rest the side of her head against his.

'What is that?' she asked.

'Don't know. It just came to me.'

June 19, 2035

A book of my selected poems came out a month ago, published by a firm that owed me a favour. A hundred-plus examples, none of them worth one of Shakespeare's toenails. No reviews, which isn't surprising. I was obsessed with poetry when young but I've had to face my limitations. The theatre's my place, especially working with someone like Amade. I understand what he needs, and he appreciates that. If you ask me, *he's* the poet. (**Ref 14**)

Reference

(Ref 14) Bridger is perceptive about his own failings as a poet. The critics – not that there were many of them – thought he had a facility for rhyming but lacked originality. On the other hand they judged his dramatic work with Amade to be of the highest order.

June 24, 2035

Location, Sharon's theatre in the Custard Factory. Amade has polished off the 'Gents toilet' scene from *The sopranos* as if it never gave him a moment's trouble, and I've been dying to see how it stands up. Given the technical difficulties involved, it was one of those occasions when I was glad not to be involved in direction. I needn't have worried – Sharon is equal to anything.

Essentially the libretto requires the five sopranos to walk through an old hotel past American tourists and spend ten minutes in the Gents toilet tarting themselves up. So most of the action takes place in a constricted space – actually, *a very constricted space*, since the girls choose to use the disabled cubicle. The audience sees the cubicle as enclosed on three sides and open on the side nearest to them. It contains a toilet bowl, wash basin, hand drier and five foot mirror. The cubicle is set within the larger Gents toilet, which has two urinals, two wash basins, two hand driers and a door through which male customers (all American) periodically enter and leave.

Sharon Adair must have taken the actors/singers through their paces several times before. Only whilst watching this first full rehearsal did I fully appreciate the scene's complexity and Sharon's talents in tackling it. I know this sounds odd because I wrote the bloody scene, but consider the following dramatic/musical considerations that had to be mastered during the course of it:

Item: The five sopranos sing in full voices except when male customers enter the larger toilet, upon which – to conceal their presence – the sopranos sing *sotto voce* and use gestures.

Item: The male customers enter singly or in pairs. If in pairs they sing in full voices.

Item: The male customers simulate using the urinals with their backs to the audience and without doing anything that will trouble the censors.

Item: When male customers activate the hand-driers (resulting in a deafening noise) the sopranos continue to imitate *sotto voce* singing, though with no sound emanating. The moment the noise of the driers ceases, the remnant of the sopranos' *sotto voce* singing bursts forth.

Item: Four of the five sopranos sing in bold, brassy voices, with accompanying gestures. The exception is Orla, whose music and singing has more pathos, and whose physique and gestures reflect her long illness.

Item: The girls change out of their school uniforms into a variety of extravagant items of costume – short skirts, blouses with buttons undone, stocking tops, G-strings, high heels, earrings. They look attractive, even erotic, but not pornographic. Someone lends Orla a Wonderbra. Orla removes a retainer brace from her mouth.

Item: The girls use various items of make-up on their faces and bodies, items that are mostly swapped around between them, including two cans of deodorant (with accompanying hisses), lipsticks, eye-liners, mascara, perfume, foundation cream, powder and nail varnish (dried under the hand-drier).

Item: the sparse facilities in the disabled cubicle have to be shared between the girls: the hand-drier, the sink, the toilet-roll, the single 5-foot mirror (one standing girl bending over, another girl squatting under).

Item: The scene ends when a male customer tries the door of the disabled cubicle and it opens. Customer: 'Well, my apology, young ladies.' A girl: 'I'm sorry, sir. We're just doing some extra swotting for the exams.'

The libretto for this scene is good – though I say it myself – but as usual I've been trumped by Amade's music. He sets up a frantic pace in the girls' singing, using all kinds of clever devices to accentuate the best lines. Set against this, often at the same time, were Orla's solos, full of sadness and passionate longing. I recalled Amade lying unconscious on his lounge floor during the composition of this piece and marvelled at what he'd achieved; there seemed to be no connection between the man's physical wretchedness and the soaring majesty of his art.

June 27, 2035

The chickens are coming home to roost. My hope was that Amade had forgotten about that daft quest to find a cor anglais player, but fat chance – where music is concerned his tenacity is legendary. I'd foolishly promised to accompany him on a safari for one of these rare creatures. Now he's holding me to it; he virtually had me pinned down on his lounge sofa this morning.

'Surely another instrument would do instead?' I bleated. 'What about a trumpet? We could find someone who plays one of them.'

'Larry, please be serious. I loathe the trumpet. And by the way the trumpet is a member of the brass family.'

'So?'

'The cor anglais is a type of oboe – a woodwind instrument.'

'Oh! We'll get an oboe then.'

'No, no, no, it must be a cor anglais. Perhaps you've never heard one. Such a mellow, plaintive tone. A cor anglais *is* Orla, Larry. It's her through and through. It echoes her voice and her very being. We absolutely must have one.' He started pacing up and down the room. 'Only thing is, where from? I do have one tip-off from someone who knew the cor anglais player in the Birmingham Symphony. He'd even visited the man's home once.'

'And how long ago was that?'

'Er...about ten years.'

'Oh that's hopeless.'

'It's a starting point.'

'This is ridiculous. And where is this phantom address exactly?'

'It's in Alum Rock.'

I'd just stood up from the sofa and I immediately sat down again. My knees had set up their own involuntary twitching motion. 'No, Martin. No way. Definitely not.'

The Alum Rock district is a byword for trouble, locally and nationally. It's an inner-city suburb with a higher population density than the rest of Brum, more young people, more ethnic minorities. A crime hot-spot notorious for drugs turf wars and gangland shootings. Newspapers no longer bother with common or garden murders in the area, though they might give a mention to something unusual like a Ku Klux Klan killing or a crucifixion. (**Ref 15**)

Amade was standing over the sofa shaking me by the shoulder. 'Come on Larry, pull yourself together.'

'*Not Alum Rock.*'

'I don't understand you. Do you want us to do this show *without* a cor anglais?'

I looked at him open-mouthed. He inhabits a different planet from the rest of us.

'All right then,' he said calmly. 'I'll go on my own.'

Connie was on the far side of the room doing a bit of unaccustomed housework. She caught my eye and slowly shook her head.

We left for Alum Rock by bus the following morning. I'd consulted a map and asked the driver to give us a shout near where we wanted to get off. He ignored me. Amade and I had deliberately dressed down for the occasion but we stood out from the other passengers like new boys on the first day at school. Ten minutes after setting off the bus broke down, so outside a pub called The Fox and Goose we waited for the next one. It arrived half full and by the time we'd pushed our way onto the top deck there were just two seats free – except that the enormous bloke with braids sitting opposite had his feet up on one of them. I waited while he took a few leisurely drags on the hand-rolled gasper that was drooping from his mouth. He finally lifted his feet from the seat, leaving a residue of who knew what on the covering.

Very occasionally Amade would reveal a surprising awareness of social circumstances, and this was one of those times. He moved very close to me and murmured from the corner of his mouth 'Just sit down'. Too bad, I was in an obstreperous mood, and pointedly started brushing the shit from the Rasta's boot off the surface of the seat. In no time the bloke was on his feet and I was all but off mine as he seized the lapel of my down-market cagoule. No-one around us took a blind bit of notice.

'Anyfing wrong wiv your seat?' the Rasta enquired, his nose next to mine, his tone not a friendly one.

It was a question to which there was no acceptable answer. I spluttered, having imbibed some smoke from the man's noxious weed. Amade jumped to his feet in token support of me and the Rasta's companion started showing an interest in him. The height difference between them was comical.

'Leave my friend Amade out of this,' I said. 'He had nothing to do with it.'

At this I was instantly shoved back onto the seat.

'*Amade*!' quoth the Rasta. 'Are we talking *Martin Amade* the musician? The man wot wrote "A rose in the garbage". *That* Amade?'

'That *was* one of mine,' Martin admitted modestly.

After that I was history, along with the shit-on-the-seat incident. They sat Amade down *between them* on the double seat, where he refused a drag of weed from the Rasta's gasper and also a sniff of some other substance, though he did tactfully accept a sip from the second bloke's hip flask. Then they all discussed Amade's music with an astonishing degree of fluency. The Rasta had several Amade recordings on his phone, though he didn't appear to have paid for them. The three men were so deep in conversation I was concerned about passing our stop – wherever that was – but the Rasta had everything in hand and courteously escorted Martin to the stairs at the right moment, for good measure dinging the bell. I tagged along behind; since the lapel-grasping incident my existence had excited no further attention.

We alighted on the main road in front of a massive fabric store. Another fabric store was next door and two more were across the road. Parked cars absorbed every inch of the kerbside. The crush of people was such that if you stood still for a moment you were all but knocked off your feet.

'That was one gigantic slice of luck,' I shouted to Amade above the hubbub.

'What d'you mean?'

'That Rasta chap. That he knew your work.'

Amade gave me a look, but it would be a while longer before I finally grasped the point. 'What's the name of the street we're after?' he asked eventually.

As it turned out the one we wanted was just off the high road – a long, soulless affair of 3-storey terraced houses. We walked a hundred yards, passing a great pile of rubbish at the roadside – smashed TV sets, old washing machines, manky sofas, dozens of things.

'They have a problem with fly-tipping,' Amade observed.

The house number we'd been seeking looked as unpromising as all the rest, but we knocked anyway. A man in his 50s answered the door, possibly east European, wearing a grubby bath robe. On that instant our 'quest' seemed as hopeless as I'd always taken it to be. Behind this bloke the hallway looked as if it hadn't been swept for many months. A network of cobwebs clung from the ceiling.

'This is a long shot,' I told him, 'But we're trying to trace a bloke who used to live here – maybe still does. All we know is he was a musician and his name's Manas.'

The man nodded. 'I'm the landlord. Manas was here all right, but that was several years ago. He had no money. Had to move down-market.'

The notion of going down-market from where we were was hard to take in. 'Do you know where he might be?' I asked.

The landlord shook his head. 'It's hopeless trying to keep track of these transients. If I hear anything I'll let you know. Leave a number.'

This meant 'Go away and stop bothering me', but I went through the motions. 'That'd be my friend Martin Amade, here. Can you leave your number, Martin.'

'Amade the composer?' For the first time the landlord perked up.

'That's me,' said Martin. 'We're looking for a cor anglais player. Manas was one.'

The landlord smiled, which at one time had seemed unlikely. 'Tell me about it. The sound carries from the second floor.' He stepped forward to shake Martin's hand, but not mine. 'Will you come in please. I know a couple of people in the music business. I'll make some calls. We may be able to track him down.'

He led us through to a small lounge, cleared some books (and a cat) off two sofas, and left us there while he went off to make his calls. Amade and I exchanged raised eyebrows.

The man was back five minutes later.

'We've got him,' he said. Amade jumped to his feet as if the Holy Grail had been spoken of. The landlord gave him a scrap of paper containing a scrawled address. 'It's a 20-minute walk from here,' he said. 'Watch your step. That's a bad part of town.'

We went to the front door. 'I can't thank you enough,' said Amade.

'It's been a privilege,' said the landlord. He shook hands with Amade and nodded towards me.

We followed the map and made our way towards the new address through an increasingly desolate landscape. On two occasions I thought there might be trouble with passers-by, but we got through unscathed. Our search ended at a terraced house situated opposite a rubbish patch. An old pram was dumped in the tiny front garden and the laburnum hedge had gone mad above a low wall. The metal gate screeched as Amade pushed it open.

I said 'My mother had an expression - "A creaking gate hangs".'

'What does that mean?' said Amade.

'It means "An old codger may groan and grumble, but he's still alive".'

'Let's hope it applies to Mr Manas,' Amade said.

The resolution of our 'quest' was surprisingly straightforward. Another moment, another landlord, this time an ebullient Sikh, who was naturally disparaging of his Bengali tenant. 'I *think* he's still alive,' he said. We heard him thumping on a first floor door – '*Mr Chatterji, visitor for you*' – before bounding downstairs again. 'He may not be familiar with the word "visitor",' he said. 'You'd better go up. See if you can get any sense from him.'

The Bengali's door was ajar. Amade knocked and pushed it open. Manas Chatterji sat blinking on the single bed in his pyjamas. He'd not shaved for many days. There was an odour of decay and neglect. Amade apologised for the intrusion, introduced me then himself.

'You are Amade!' the man said.

'Martin Amade. I'm a composer.'

'I know that.'

Of course he knew! Was there anyone in Alum Rock who *didn't*?

'But why...'

Amade explained why we were there. A production of 'The sopranos'. We wanted a cor anglais player. We wanted Manas Chatterji. In this production the cor anglais shadowed the main role, etc, etc. He started to get too technical and I restrained him. I had the impression Chatterji hadn't communicated with other people for a long time. He was like a baby learning to walk, taking his first few steps.

'I don't know...' Chatterji was mumbling. 'Long time...'

'*Can* you still play?' urged Amade.

'I...maybe...you know what they say...riding a bicycle...'

'That's the spirit,' cried Amade. I put out a hand to restrain him.

'Mr Chatterji,' I asked. 'Do you still have an instrument?' I'd been looking round and the room was almost bare of possessions. 'Do you still own a cor anglais?'

Chatterji considered the question. By now I was getting used to the rhythms of this conversation, which was like a long-distance phone call with a delay on the line.

'Wait,' the man said eventually.

In slow motion he rose from the bed and dragged his only chair across to the wardrobe, climbed precariously onto it and fumbled about on top till he'd laid hands on a package wrapped in newspaper. It added to the unreality of the scene, I thought afterwards, that we just stood and watched without offering to help. He handed the package down to Amade. Back at ground level Chatterji resumed his place on the bed. The browning newspaper fell apart in his hands, revealing a long, thin instrument with a peach-shaped bell at one end. He appeared to revive a bit with this thing in his hands and now started blowing at the other end, but all he got was a series of squeaks with the odd note in between. The man now produced a little tin box from the remnants of the newspaper, took a couple of small squares from it, and fitted them into the mouthpiece of his instrument. If anything he reminded me of a fisherman putting a new bait onto a hook. (**Ref 16**)

'Oboists and their reeds, eh,' remarked Amade.

'The very devil,' croaked Chatterji.

'Twin reeds,' Amade said to me, with a nod of his head.

I let him prattle on. You have to, with musicians.

Finally the Bengali had fiddled enough to his satisfaction. He rose and signalled for us to sit on the bed while he parked himself in the chair.

Then he began to play.

There were a few squeaks at first, but as he warmed to his task the rich, individual sound of the cor anglais (precisely as described by Amade earlier) came through loud and clear. I saw at once that this could be Orla; I visualised Nancy Stourage treading the boards at the Custard Factory with this sweet music mirroring her every step. It was an extraordinary experience sitting in a wretched room amidst the unsavoury ruins of Chatterji's bed, hearing this perfect sound emanating from the sad creature before us. By the time he'd finished I was holding my breath.

There was complete silence for a moment. Then Chatterji said 'You know the piece?'

'"The swan of Tuonela",' said Amade.

They both had tears running down their silly faces. Musicians!

There was a brief pause during which both men composed themselves, before Amade spoke. 'It is wonderful to hear the sound of that instrument again, and so beautifully played. So, Mr Chatterji, I would like to ask you formally. Will you play for us in the rehearsals and performances of *The sopranos* at the Custard Factory theatre? You will be part of a 12-person orchestra.'

The Bengali began to tremble. 'I don't know. Do you think I could do that?'

'If you can play the way you just have after such a long lay-off – then yes, I am sure you can.'

Chatterji took a deep breath. 'I want to do it, but you are taking a big risk. I will give my services free.'

'You will be paid the same rate as everyone else.' Amade dug into his pocket and handed over some banknotes. 'Here is an advance.' This struck an odd note since Amade had little enough to give away. 'You need to get fit again. Go for walks. Practice your instrument regularly. And you must eat properly. Start slowly, and work up to a butter chicken with peshwari nan, or some other gut-rot Bengali recipe. Do all these things. I'm relying on you.'

Now Chatterji surprised us by jumping to his feet and pulling on a pair of trousers over his pyjamas. 'This calls for a celebration,' he said. 'I have some green tea somewhere. I shall borrow a couple of mugs from the landlord. We'll boil up some water in his kitchen.'

'I'll help you,' said Amade, and they went down together.

The recuperation of Manas Chatterjee had begun.

Ten minutes later we sat in his room drinking green tea. Not the most riotous celebration but it was a step on the way. There was no table, and mugs were unsteadily balanced on the bed. Amade and I had smart

Birmingham City mugs borrowed from the landlord; Manas had a sorry affair chipped in several places. He'd revived quite touchingly compared to the moment when we first set eyes on him. He became almost garrulous, as if the green tea had achieved an alcoholic effect.

'We Bengalis have a talent for the arts,' he said. 'Practical matters – mending a fuse, changing a plug – not so good, but a long tradition in artistic disciplines.'

Amade asked how his family had originally come to Britain.

'My father fled to England during the Bangladesh war and settled in the Birmingham area. He proposed to my mother on the Saltley Viaduct near here.' Again there was a reference to the artistic background. 'One of his ancestors was a music hall singer who helped to popularise the Victorian song "Come into the garden, Maud".'

How much of this to believe, how he had come to his present sorry circumstances, we could not know. What we did know was that he could play the cor anglais.

An hour later, as we stepped down from our vehicle at Birmingham bus station following a mercifully uneventful ride, Amade asked me, 'Well Larry – was it worth it?'

'You tell me,' I replied.

References

(Ref 15) The unsavoury elements of Alum Rock are what get highlighted in the news, but to be fair, most residents seem to like living there. A frequent comment of the locals is that all facilities are within walking distance – shops, doctors' surgeries, dentists, the Heartlands Hospital. There are three train stations – Adderley Park, Duddeston and Stechford – two gyms, six primary schools and three secondaries, and a busy high street which contains an enormous Islamic store.

(Ref 16) The cor anglais – literally, the 'English horn' – is considered to be the tenor member of the oboe family. The two reeds fit one on top of the other in the mouthpiece. The rich tone over a two and a half octave range allows the instrument to excel in the interpretation of slow and expressive melodies. It only became a regular member of the orchestra from the time of Wagner onwards. (Information from Wikipedia)

July 21, 2035

Connie recently observed that her husband's workload has boiled down to two things: *The sopranos*, and the mysterious commission for a vampire oratorio. Oddly enough, my own schedule is heading in the same direction, because Amade has asked *me* to contribute to the oratorio.

   The way this oratorio is being commissioned and paid for doesn't resemble anything I've experienced before. The 'dark messenger' (as Connie calls him) who first turned up at New Street station has now reappeared while Amade was taking his morning constitutional into Moseley centre. The man enquired about the oratorio, accepted Amade's progress report and again handed over money. This sort of money is hard to refuse, as even Connie admits. She bitterly resents the effect vampires are having on Amade's mental health, but she can now afford to heat the house properly and has bought a winter coat (albeit at a charity shop). When and where – and if ever – the oratorio will be performed interests her less than it does Amade.

   I struggle to get my head round oratorios, since they're usually associated with religious subjects. Let's face it, if I'm involved you're unlikely to get the *St Matthew Passion* or *The dream of Gerontius*. To bring to mind the genuine Dracula story I've returned to the original Bram Stoker novel – published in 1897! - which has since been masked by countless naff film treatments. Amade and I have made various changes to the plot: our 45-minute version is set in Essex, not Transylvania, and we've reduced the number of named characters; on the other hand we've greatly increased the number of vampires!

In our chorus the usual combinations of singers will be followed:

> Tenors (representing the forces of sweetness and light)
>
> Basses (representing vampires)
>
> Sopranos and altos (all vampires)

There will also be five soloists, representing the novel's main characters, and reflecting five different voice ranges.

An advantage of the sponsor's generous funding is that Amade can hire a few singers at knock-down prices to rehearse certain passages. Today I'd been invited to attend one of these events. The singers present were:

> A tenor, playing Jonathan Harker, a young solicitor
>
> A soprano, playing Lucy, a friend of Harker's fiancée
>
> Three sopranos from the chorus of vampires

And who was the singer playing Lucy? None other than our old friend Nancy Stourage from *The sopranos*, appearing in a different manifestation.

Something odd happened early on. As I arrived Connie offered me coffee, which I declined. This subject came up again shortly afterwards. Amade had his singers lined up ready to start when he unexpectedly asked me to declaim some lines from literature to set the tone. I gave him a passage from *Hamlet*:

> *'Tis now the very witching time of night*

When churchyards yawn and hell itself breathes out

Contagion to this world. Now could I drink hot blood

And do such bitter business as the day

Would quake to look on.'

Connie was crossing the room as I spoke and piped up 'Larry, I did ask if you wanted anything to drink'. She looked surprised when the four sopranos set up a cackling to rival the witches from *Macbeth*. Connie doesn't really have a sense of humour, so I assume she just wasn't paying attention. She exited left, peeved to have been the butt of other people's derision.

   Then Amade started to play. As always, since that first evening at The Electric, I was overwhelmed by his music. Initially this weaved its magic behind a conventional conversation, as the solicitor expressed concern about Lucy's health problems and she assured him she was doing OK. But unknown to Harker, Lucy had already been fatally infected with the vampire's curse, and suddenly the tone changed. Everything Lucy said contained an element of threat and the solicitor became alarmed. The full horror of the girl's situation now broke out. Stourage, so sweet and vulnerable in the role of Orla, became a macabre sight, arching her body over Harker like a snake ready to strike, while her features turned to a disturbing mask and her lips drew back from menacing teeth (whilst she contrived at the same time to sing). Her voice, capable of such sweetness, had become a screech that nevertheless negotiated several octaves with perfect musicality. I felt relieved not to be in Harker's shoes, and indeed the young tenor cowered away from this shrieking harpie in a way that suggested genuine fear.

   Amade's music hereabouts was his and yet not his. He was incapable of writing in bad taste but this passage combined half-familiar harmonies with some hideous discords. The composer didn't look himself as he crouched over the keyboard, teeth bared, all traces of his customary mild manner abandoned. Shivers ran up the back of my neck. Now the three girls from the chorus joined the fray, all angularity and frenetic gestures, screeching in unison with Stourage or howling abrasively against her. I tried to imagine what Amade would come up with when the chorus of two dozen male and female vampires were in full cry, and shivered again.

'They fucking terrify me.'

It was Connie's voice. I heard it at the precise moment I became aware of her presence, very close, emitting the earthy tang that is unlike anyone else's.

'It's all death, death, death,' she said, in an abrasive low voice. 'How can he write such things?'

'It's his job.'

'Well I wish he wouldn't. I wish he'd never met that sodding messenger. The man can keep his money.'

She left with the same economy of movement that had graced her arrival, off to prepare refreshments for the singers. Soon afterwards Amade brought the proceedings to a temporary halt. He urged the singers to a tremendous climax whilst pounding the piano like a maniac. Then three things happened in quick succession: the four vampires shrieked 'Kill, kill, kill, kill, kill' on a repeated top-A note; Amade leapt to his feet shouting 'Tea break'; the singers broke into a giant cackle of laughter, falling about and clutching each other in mirth.

I went over to discuss something with Amade at the piano, so was late joining the performers at their tea. Connie had them sitting round the big wooden table in the kitchen, on which were a couple of teapots, plus plates of cakes and scones. I plonked myself down next to Nancy Stourage and was about to commend her rendering of the tormented vampire when she turned to the girl next to her.

'Helen, you've just taken the last scone.'

'I know,' Helen agreed. 'They're delicious.'

'That's not the point,' said Stourage. '*I* wanted it.'

Helen was unabashed. 'You're too late pardner – I've got it. Have one of the cakes instead, why don't you. There's plenty of them left.'

'But I wanted the scone,' Stourage persisted. She didn't actually stamp her foot, but the tone of voice was consistent with foot-stamping. Those sweet features of hers had contorted disagreeably. The other sopranos were grinning, enjoying the little contretemps. 'I have the main part,' insisted Stourage, 'So I should have the scone if I want it.'

'If only I'd known,' said Helen. 'Hold on, there might be just a chance of your getting some...' So saying, she wolfed down the final remnants. 'No, no, sorry, too late – it's all gone.'

Stourage was on her feet, purple-faced, too furious to bark more than a few inarticulate phrases. She ran from the room. The sopranos grinned some more.

During the remainder of the rehearsal I sat pondering the transformation of Stourage from golden girl to spoilt brat. I of all people should not have been surprised. My entire professional life has been dogged by the witless antics of the acting profession. 'Actors – no wonder the church buries them at night,' ran a line from some French movie I saw aeons ago. (**Ref 17**) For some reason – god knows why – it's too much to expect one individual both to portray the human virtues and to exemplify them. I wondered if Amade might take a different view. Perhaps he'd figure that to master perfect pitch and sweetness of tone was enough from the exponents of *his* art. Then I remembered his pitiless, almost childlike grasp of the highs and lows in human nature, and decided to leave the subject alone. It was giving me a headache.

Reference

(Ref 17) The line about actors comes from Marcel Carne's film 'Les enfants du paradis' (1945). Screenplay by Jacques Prevert.

August 8, 2035

Another spell at Amade's place working on *The sopranos*. It's coming along, I hope. When you're developing something the moments of exhilaration come against a nagging background of worry: is the structure of the piece right?; will it cut the mustard with the few remaining followers of serious music?; can Amade and I combine our efforts so that the joins don't show?

   Connie wasn't in town, and this got me thinking how often those two are apart. Amade has travelled a great deal in his short life but he's had to slow down, mainly due to ill health. Now Connie's the one who moves about. She's addicted to health spas, never mind that she's already in robust physical health. She'll try out any new place that offers posh gyms, pedicures, sun lamps, moisturising, mud baths, all kinds of massage. The place she's patronising at this moment, in Wolverhampton, is run by a Hindu guru type. I saw their brochures, which are hot on diets and bowel movements. The patrons probably end up drinking their own piss.

   I got an insight into the relationship of the Amade love-birds when I went off for a pee of my own in their house. Coming back from the bog you pass the famous snooker room, and I couldn't resist going in. Amade's computer was on a small table in the corner. For once he had a power supply going (thank you, dark messenger) and a half-finished email to his wife was on the screen. I shouldn't have looked at it, but of course I did. My eye was caught by the opening salutation, 'Dear Pussy Wussy', and I read on in surprise and amusement. I know Amade lacked a formal education because he told me so himself. He'd been tutored at home by his father, a common enough practice since the quality of state schools plummeted so alarmingly. As a consequence the composer's spelling often goes awry and his grammar is distinctly unreliable. (Of course these features contrast with Amade's musical literacy, which is utterly beyond reproach.)

The striking element of the snooker room email was the personal play language Amade lapsed into with his missus. I can't remember it word for word, but there was a lot of 'hoping that pussy has trimmed her whiskers nicely' and 'hoping that pussy has not gone out at night on her own', plus a punning sequence to the effect that 'your a-miewsing observations have given Mr Tomcat paws for thought'. Such language was a far cry from anything I'd heard from them in the house. No doubt Amade was falling back on a private form of communication from their early days together. Even so it struck an odd note given their current realities: an impecunious, ailing husband with a demanding and sexually active wife. What came over most powerfully was Amade's anxiety about his wife's behaviour in public, which he clearly feels is unseemly for a married woman.

In one passage he threatened to give Connie 'a nice spanking' if she failed to follow his guidance, which gives further insight into their early married life. Not that I could envisage Amade administering a spanking now, but I could damn well imagine Connie receiving one, *and* asking for more.

August 22, 2035

Today I've an irresistible impulse to confide to the diary some elements of my love life. This isn't easy. I freely admit to my reputation as a man susceptible to the opposite sex. Yes, there have been moments of weakness when I unwisely succumbed to a passing temptation. But the full truth is different from my public image. I'm a man whose main romantic attachments have been long-term and who, once attracted to someone, will move heaven and earth to sustain the relationship. (**Ref 18**) Up to now my life has seen two such attachments and I recently embarked upon a third. The pen that is now trembling in my fingers testifies to the power of this new liaison. But I'm also acutely aware of the risks involved in making this diary entry. Should the lady in question witness even the mildest criticism of her character, I'm in deep trouble. And the mention of two previous attachments could lead to weeks of tantrums and the probability of physical violence. (**Ref 19**)

The name of this new love is Adriana Gabriel, though she is known as La Mancuna because of her birth in Manchester. She is an actor and above all a singer, and I refer to her ladyship now because I'm pressing her case for a role in *The sopranos*. I've finished the libretto for the opera's final scenes, and Amade – working flat out as usual – has come up with the music. One scene concerns the moment when the five sopranos and the rest of the choir arrive at the Edinburgh rehearsal hall after various adventures in the city. Presiding over the rehearsal are two nuns, one of whom – Sister Comden – is the role coveted by Adriana.

A limitation of the *modus operandi* that Amade and Sharon Adair adopted – that is, writing and rehearsing *The sopranos* 'as we go along' – is that we've had to cast it piecemeal. Casting decisions are made jointly by Amade, myself and Sharon. We met in the Custard Factory theatre today to allocate the last tranche of parts, including that of Sister Comden. I submitted my proposal for Adriana Gabriel.

'Oh, you mean La Mancuna,' exclaimed Amade.

I should have guessed that Amade would have come across a singer of her quality. It helps – and it doesn't help – that the two of them know each other. It helps – and doesn't help – that Sharon Adair *hasn't* met La Mancuna.

'I ought to declare an interest,' I said. 'La Mancuna and I are romantically involved.'

'Oh lumme,' said Adair. 'That's torn it.'

I turned to Amade. 'So you know the woman. What's your opinion of her musical talent?'

'Oh that's easy. She's an exceptional vocalist with an extraordinary range. She can handle a top E with ease, and make it sound completely natural. In my experience audiences like her.'

'What does she look like?' asked Adair.

Amade hesitated. 'Her figure...a little heavy, perhaps.'

'Which should not preclude her playing a middle-aged nun,' I pointed out.

'Can she act?' Adair persisted.

'She's so-so,' said Amade. 'I'd take her for the singing. It's really outstanding.'

'Does she get on with people?' said Adair.

'Ah...' said Amade.

Adair turned to me. 'Larry?'

'Oh you know these artistic types,' I said. 'They all indulge in a spot of temperament now and then.'

'Forgive me, Larry.' Adair was remorseless. 'I mean, does she even get on with *you*?'

'A bit up and down,' I admitted. 'Last week we had a row about my teeth.'

'Your *teeth*?'

'She doesn't like them. I don't blame her. I've had my problems in that respect.' (**Ref 20**)

'Decision time.' Adair was all businesslike. 'This is an opera, so Martin – you have the casting vote.'

'In that case, let's take her,' said Amade. 'She really does sing like an angel.'

I concealed a sigh of relief. La Mancuna *is* a wonderful singer, but as a lover she's jealous as hell. I've not seen how she conducts herself in a dressing room but she once took a dislike to my landlady, a sedate dress-maker in her early 50s, and punched one of her tailor's dummies to the ground. She's never set eyes on the 16-year old daughter Angelique, thank god. I made sure of that at least.

All in all, I think I've got off lightly. Adriana will be delighted to have landed the role, and I'll be handsomely rewarded between the sheets. As for *The sopranos*...well, I can surely keep her on track during the rehearsals.

References

(Ref 18) By all accounts Bridger is soft-pedalling these early relationships. In truth he had a history of falling into the clutches of possessive, tenacious women who made his life hell.

(Ref 19) It seems probable that La Mancuna did indeed get a sight of Bridger's diary. The relevant page of the journal has been torn into several pieces and crudely repaired with cellotape.

(Ref 20) Bridger is also downplaying his dental problems. Years earlier, one of his enemies had advised the application of nitric acid to cure an abscess. This caused Bridger's teeth to fall out and destroyed both his

digestive system and his appetite.

September 1, 2035

La Mancuna attended her first rehearsal a week later in the Custard Factory theatre. She played the role of the nun, Sister Comden, alongside a second nun called Sister Fagan. Also present were the 12 members of the choir – the five 'sopranos' of the title plus seven other girls. And also on parade were Sharon Adair, Amade and myself.

In this scene the stage represented the Edinburgh hall where rehearsals took place for all choirs participating in the competition. The girls from Our Lady of Perpetual Succour school had an afternoon rehearsal slot and were supposed to be there by 4pm, following several free hours to explore the city. As the scene opened Sisters Comden and Fagan were addressing eight of the girls, all neatly dressed in the school uniform of blazers, ties and respectable skirts.

'Four of our girls are missing,' sang Sister Fagan.

'Four girls are missing,' echoed Sister Comden. 'Where are they? Where are these girls?'

The other eight shrugged in unison. 'We don't know where,' they sang.

Two girls called Fionnula and Kay now entered, both wearing the school uniform.

'Sorry we're late, Sisters,' sang Fionnula. 'Kay and I got lost. Kay isn't feeling well.'

Kay smiled, then turned and vomited onto the floor. The rest of the choir gasped. Sister Fagan covered her eyes with her hands. Kay spat into the little pile of vomit.

Now the other missing girls – Orla and Amanda – appeared on the fringes of the hall. Amanda was first, carrying a large shopping bag that concealed her body below the waist. Orla was behind her, with another shopping bag in place. Amanda sang 'We're sorry Sister Condom, but our uniforms have been stolen.' Another concerted gasp from the choir.

Nancy Stourage, playing Orla, clarified. 'We weren't wearing them at the time.'

Both girls moved the carrier bags aside to reveal extremely short skirts that were barely skirts at all; beside the girls in school uniforms their legs seemed obscenely exposed. More gasps from the company.

Orla sang 'Sorry, Sister Condom, we were trying on these clothes in a shop and someone stole our school uniforms.

Sister Comden made a show of fainting to the ground. The intention was that four of the girls, Orla amongst them, would intervene to break her fall, but La Mancuna was too heavy for them. Superimposed upon her stocky figure was a sizeable paunch that swung from side to side. She was sweating heavily and clearly hadn't bothered to use a deodorant. Her body slipped through the girls' fingers and hit the wooden floor with a thwack.

Sharon Adair, who'd been standing in the body of the theatre, ran towards the footlights. 'Girls, get into position earlier. You mustn't let Sister Comden hit the ground.'

'But she's too heavy,' complained one of the girls, wrinkling her nose in distaste.

'Sister Condom needs to lose weight,' cried Nancy Stourage, playing Orla.

La Mancuna was on her feet again, staring blackly in Orla's direction.

It was immediately apparent that these two women weren't going to get on. In some ways they were similar – with eyes to die for, shapely sets of lips, and both possessed of extravagant voices that stood out from the crowd. But La Mancuna had formed an immediate dislike, which she didn't bother to conceal. She took a step towards her rival.

'You stupid girl.'

There was the sharp sound of a blow, and it took the company a moment to realise that La Mancuna had slapped Nancy Stourage in the face.

Sharon Adair rapped her knuckles on the stage. 'Hey, hey, Adriana...'

'I'm known as La Mancuna,' came the response.

'That's too high-falutin' for me,' said Adair. 'You'll be Adriana and like it. And note this well – there will be no physical contact between actors on stage unless I say so. Any more antics like that and you'll get your marching orders, glorious voice or no.'

'And I don't want people calling me a condom,' continued La Mancuna.

'It's in the script,' said Adair. 'The girls have to get the nun's name wrong deliberately.'

'Not when she's talking to me as me.'

'I was just trying hard to keep in character,' La Stourage offered sweetly. The smile hadn't left her face, which infuriated La Mancuna all the more. Of course I'd seen Stourage in cankanterous mood before, never mind the angelic appearance; she could be a gold-plated bitch at times.

'Just stick to the script,' said Adair, getting low on patience. 'Carry on, Adriana. Take it from your speech about the perils of the city.' La Mancuna instantly picked up her place in the script. She had a memory for lines, if only she could control her emotions. She told the girl Kay that she was too ill to sing ('I believe you have been in contact with alcohol') and that she was to swap her attire with Orla. As for Amanda, she 'couldn't go on if her uniform was really lost.' She threatened 'severe punishments' for the girls who had transgressed. Kay went to lie down across two upright chairs and Amanda came on stage with a bucket and mop to clear up Kay's spew.

'Now listen carefully,' Comden began, moving into a passionately sung peroration. 'I see some of you have ignored my advice about staying clear of the shopping centre. That place is out of bounds to you all. Drugs gangs operate there, intent on corrupting innocent schoolgirls. From now on you are to move around in groups. Do now allow yourselves to become separated. Men are watching all the time. Wicked, wicked men. Listen to what I say. Men are watching all the time. Wicked, wicked men...'

As she sang, the ten schoolgirls – eight in uniform and two in very short skirts – echoed the words 'Wicked, wicked men,' and 'Men are watching all the time', over and over in the form of a choral background. Sister Comden's voice rose above them, then swooped downwards again. It made for a most lovely sound, and the woman's glittering eyes – heavily made up despite her nun-hood – enhanced the effect. In a few brief minutes La Mancuna had illustrated why she could secure big operatic roles and why she was unsuited to any roles at all.

When she sang 'Wicked, wicked men' Orla, still in the shortest of skirts, moved her hips in a simulation of sexual intercourse.

As the final notes died down Sharon Adair said 'Orla, don't do that'.

I'd not seen hair or hide of Amade throughout the rehearsal, but I heard his music and that was enough.

September 8, 2035

Wouldn't you know it, La Mancuna has blamed *me* for her embarrassments at the *Sopranos* rehearsal, in particular for being bested by Stourage before half the cast. So instead of sharing an intimate weekend with the blasted woman, basking in her approval, I'm in the dog-house. Nothing to do then but fall back on my own resources and reflect on the world around me, which in these dog days is a certain recipe for depression.

   Some of this is simple nostalgia. I can tolerate the physical limitations of our 2035 world but like other men of my years I've memories of better times, of hopes and expectations, of a more robust planet. I miss things that I never expected to miss: the *winter*, the bare branches of trees, the sensation of ice under-foot, of passing from a chilled landscape to sit before a log fire.

   Even those experiences cannot match the lost world of human discourse that people of my occupation naturally hold dear. Thank god we are past the worst excesses of what were called social media: the reliance on a 6x4-inch device that promised much and delivered little; the *inwardness* of communication, with our vast store of inheritance mislaid; the subjugation of intellect to habit and the mindless tropes of the advertising fraternity; the Neanderthal postures of people walking the streets, recycling bland intelligence as if their little lives depended upon it. What remains now lacks all vitality; even our sense of loss is dulled. Our best shot at creativity is reserved for pornography, which gropes into the interstices of every hearth and home. It cannot be long before the whole crumbling structure comes crashing down and the streets are peopled by zombies.

   I'm acutely aware of my own good fortune in this wilderness. Through luck and no particular judgement I drifted into the creative world, where even the lamest products must contain the seeds of renewal. In the past few months I've come to know a man who rises above the ant-hill of daily existence to aim for the stars, and drags me kicking and screaming in his wake; a man who cares nothing for fame or notoriety yet garners both along the way. Should our planet's miserable remains be disinterred one day by scholars from a future civilization, my own name may feature as a footnote to Amade's dazzling legacy.

September 24, 2035

A phone call from Connie. The 'dark messenger' – as she insists on calling him – is back again. This time he turned up bold as brass at their house and hammered on the front door. Connie caught a glimpse of his sombre form through the window and cowered out of sight. For a no-nonsense type of woman she's letting this whole episode get to her; she said the three loud knocks on their door sounded like a summons from the underworld. Hah! And she's the practical one! Amade, an artist, don't forget (and we know all about them) has mentally embroidered the affair to a point that's driving his wife to distraction. He's convinced himself that appearances by the dark messenger presage his own death. I told him 'Don't be ridiculous. Would a man who wanted you dead throw money at you?' – for the lavish payments keep coming. But there's no arguing with Amade in this mood. Yesterday he saw three black cats during his morning constitutional and fell into an awful tizzy. He works all hours on the vampire score and cannot be persuaded to rest. The man is on the edge of losing his reason. He seems to believe that by some weird alchemy the vampire's curse has entered his own blood stream. Yesterday Connie approached him with Bram Stoker's original book in hand crying 'Look, it's just a story, that's all. It's just a bloody book,' and threw the offending volume at the wall. To no avail.

   The vampire rehearsals, conducted with hired personnel, have continued apace. The vocalists buy wholeheartedly into Amade's vision, singing with a frenzy that has brought complaints from the neighbours. Nancy Stourage embraces her role with such abandon that fellow singers won't stand next to her. And when she left the house one dark evening having forgotten to remove her vampire teeth, a passer-by caught sight of this apparition and fled howling down the street.

To be Connie's confidant in these matters is an uncomfortable experience. I'm concerned about Amade's health of course – and Connie's, for that matter – but I also worry about his musical priorities. The first performance of *The sopranos* is a mere two weeks away, and Amade's attention is being seduced away by the insidious, dark charm of another subject altogether. We shall soon know the worst.

September 27, 2035

Another phone call I could have done without, this time from Sharon Adair. I've been nagging her about one of the final scenes in *The sopranos*. In it the sickly Orla, back at school, anticipates a visit from a young bloke she met in an Edinburgh bar. She intends to take him onto the hillside overlooking the bay and enjoy her first experience of sexual intercourse. Coincidentally, Alan Warner's original novel has a nuclear submarine 'parked' out in the bay, which is important to the plot because the girls like to chat up sailors from the sub in local pubs. So during Orla's 'first time' the randy couple hear a hissing sound and see that 'the conning tower of the submarine was driving through the narrow inlet, its huge, sucking presence swinging around as it moved awaywards'. I really liked this conjunction of events and thought it would make for a wonderful consummation of the whole event. Amade has already written some stirring music for it. However Sharon's phone call brought disappointing news.

'I've been agonising over this submarine business, Larry.'

'I don't like the sound of "agonising",' I told her.

'Well that's just it. I've been over this from every angle and it's a technical nightmare. If we did it properly – and I wouldn't contemplate any other way – it would cost a fortune. We can't afford it. I'm so sorry, Larry, it's economics. I just can't risk running this event at a loss.'

Normally I'd have thrown a mega-tantrum at this point, and it was a mark of my respect for Sharon Adair that I kept myself in check. 'That's a great pity,' I told her. 'I know you'd do it if you could. Thank you for telling me.'

She apologised again and rang off.

I launched a savage kick at my waste paper bin, which skidded across the room scattering rubbish in its wake.

October 10, 2035

I'm writing this in my room at 2am after the first performance of *The sopranos*. I am a happy man. On rare occasions in my life circumstances have conspired to bring about a memorable experience, when everything comes out as I want it to. This was one of those occasions.

Most unusually, the weather was on its best behaviour. The stifling cloud cover that now chaperones our daily lives inexplicably gave way to pleasant sunlight. Before the show, singers and instrumentalists alike sat round wooden tables in the open area behind the Custard Factory theatre, while staff circulated with cold drinks and snacks. Amade was nervous – his usual demeanour before a performance – but the vampire fever had drained from his person. Connie nodded towards her husband's small figure as he paced around the tables and gave me a quick thumbs-up.

Sharon Adair moved among the company distributing copies of a playbill she'd designed for the occasion. It read:

'The singers and players of the Custard Factory theatre have the honour to perform

for the first time

The Sopranos

A musical entertainment written by Larry Bridger, from the novel by Alan Warner.

Music is by the distinguished composer Martin Amade who will, out of respect

for a gracious public and friendship for the writer of the piece, conduct the orchestra

himself.'

There followed the names and roles of the singers, then a list of the musicians with their instruments. (**Ref 21**)

I went across to the table where a batch of six musicians included Manas Chatterji, the cor anglais player whom Amade and I had disinterred from his Alum Rock bedsit. I'd barely recognised the man, who was very different from the crumbling, pyjama-clad figure of our first meeting. His features had filled out and his manner was unassuming rather than diffident. He told me *The sopranos* had been a life-changing experience. I had the impression the other musicians, younger than Chatterji, were keeping an eye open for his welfare.

When the time came I walked round to the theatre entrance with

Amade and Sharon Adair. At which point Amade and I got a big surprise, because both the foyer and the forecourt outside were seething with people; a highly unusual sight in the theatrical world of 2035.

'God Sharon, you're going to be sold out,' I said.

'And then some,' she replied. 'Same thing for the other nights. There'll be people standing along the back.'

'How did you do it?'

She nodded towards our companion. 'With a really top artist there usually comes a point when a reputation takes off.' She linked an arm companionably with mine. 'Plus your own contribution, of course.'

Amade and I spoke in unison. 'And yours.'

The atmosphere of the foyer – that indefinable air of suppressed excitement that every director wants to hear (and rarely does) – had transmitted itself to the auditorium. I soaked it up from my seat in the third row where (unlike Sharon Adair) I could remain incognito. Many of those present were under 40, unlike the collection of ancients I'd witnessed at the Snape Maltings theatre. I heard Amade's name bandied about, but no mention of my own except for a 'Who's this Bridger cove?' from two rows behind.

As she likes to do, Sharon Adair staged a surprise – a surprise even to the script-writer. Theatregoers hadn't quite settled into their seats when an altercation sprang up in the front row. Three young women began a heated argument that seemed unbecoming for a theatrical opening night. One of them shrieked 'You silly bitch', and got her face slapped. Then I noticed that the girls were in school uniform. All three ran giggling up some steps onto the stage. The curtain rose, a strident chord came from the orchestra, the audience laughed and we were away.

There is a point in any show when audience reaction alerts you to the prospect of success (or utter failure). In our case it was the scene where Orla, in hospital, has her first stab at sexual intercourse, albeit with a dying Norwegian sailor in the next bed. Nancy Stourage's Orla conveyed the neediness and longing of the sick girl so passionately that even my beady eyes filled with tears. The orchestra was seated at the back of the stage behind a gauze curtain, and I saw Manas Chatterji rise to weave a beguiling counterpart to Nancy's voice on his cor anglais. Amade, baton in hand, was bent almost double, as if his own exertions could amplify the music.

Then Orla began her physical assault upon the unconscious sailor. The gasps from the audience were as nothing beside their reaction when the dying man rose from his bed bellowing inchoate noises, sending a drip stand flying (' blood everywhere', as Sharon Adair had promised), with Orla wailing in fear and compassion and the orchestra going bananas. More consternation from the stalls and hands clapped to foreheads, but there also came (oh wonderful, how wonderful) waves of laughter. How did I feel about an audience that was torn by such conflicting emotions? I felt absolutely fucking amazing. I felt like a king.

A good feature of this script – though I say it myself – is the variety of different situations, which keep the audience guessing. We soon reached the scene where five sopranos crowded into the gents toilet of an old hotel – no, make that *the disabled cubicle* of the gents toilet – to change into come-hither clothing and plaster their virginal features with make-up. The unusual toilet set drew applause when it was first revealed, but most of it stayed empty once the girls were in the cubicle, except when American tourists doddered in to piss at the urinals, wash their hands at the sink, or dry them at the (very noisy) hand-dryers.

Now Sharon Adair's genius was displayed in all its sundry ramifications. Sharon was sent to earth to rehearse actors, which was fortunate because the frantic cubicle action, egged on by Amade's dashing score, required split-second timing. The handling of props is a nightmare for directors, and here the girls had to juggle with costumes, 5-inch heels, suspenders, Wonderbras, earrings, lipsticks, nail varnish, mascara and unravelling toilet rolls. They competed and cooperated, were funny, sad (in Orla's case), loud, erotic and ridiculous. Timing was especially crucial when old blokes entered the main body of the toilet, at which point the girls' voices sank to a barely audible sotto voce, regaining full volume as the men left the scene; or when hand-dryers blotted out all other sounds and the singing had to resume as soon as the dryers fell silent. The scene ended when an old guy on crutches tried the door of the disabled cubicle; it opened onto a tableau of sweet young girls, a picture of innocence belied by their minuscule skirts and vampishly painted faces.

When the interval came along I refrained from going back-stage. Amade would be jumpy, Sharon busy, and the singers locked into the delicate web of relationships that affected any cast mid-performance. Instead I stretched my legs down the aisle and luxuriated in the sweet smell of success.

The second half begins with a series of situations involving girls in the big city, most of these moments fairly restrained, as character is established amongst the leading players. But all hell broke loose in the scene where the schoolgirls assembled for a final rehearsal under the direction of Sisters Comden and Fagan. At first only eight girls were present, properly dressed in their school uniforms. Then Kay and Fionnula turned up but Kay (who'd been drinking) vomited on the floor. Finally Orla and Amanda appeared, luridly dressed in very short skirts.

I had completely forgotten Sharon's story of the stage manager owning a cat that sometimes trod the boards – or perhaps my subconscious refused to admit it. Now, sure enough, the cat – an unkempt ginger affair – chose this moment to come on stage. The audience responded immediately. Maybe some of them knew of the legend, because there were murmurs of 'The cat', 'The cat' all around. Others leant forward in their seats, surprised or amazed or intrigued, even imagining that the cat's appearance was a deliberate element of the show. The wretched animal strolled right past the ten girls in school uniforms but paused before Orla and Amanda, staring critically up at their minuscule skirts and the expanse of leg revealed. It drew a few titters from the stalls, but worse was to follow.

To simulate the act of spewing on stage is always a challenge, and I happened to know that the 'Kay' character had managed it by taking a mouthful of Weetabix and milk before walking on. When the ginger moggie reached the pile of 'vomit' he stopped and took a moment to lap it up. The audience reaction was predictable, but singers were also affected. La Mancuna, playing Sister Comden, had been out of sorts all evening and didn't disguise her fury at the turn of events. I hoped things would settle down because the cat then finished its perambulation and, finding nothing else of interest, exited stage right to a ripple of applause.

Sadly there was more to incur La Mancuna's displeasure. We'd reached the moment when Nancy Stourage addressed her enemy as 'Sister Condom'. The bad blood between Stourage and La Mancuna was manifest, and Stourage spoke in a voice dripping with contempt. There was no come-back for La Mancuna because the script called for her to fall down in a faint, whereupon she was supposed to be caught by three of the girls before hitting the ground. Instead Stourage made a big show of struggling with La Mancuna's weight, and the whole choir crowded round to help. It didn't help that La Mancuna's overblown figure was unsuited to a nun's habit, so that her heavy breasts swung about like wrecking balls under the thin fabric; truth to tell I've been struck a few glancing blows by them myself. But now La Stourage went too far, with an unscripted cry of 'Crikey – the woman weighs a ton'.

Audience laughs are one of the theatre's eternal mysteries; someone should write a thesis on the subject. There's no reason why a line should on one night be greeted by complete silence and the next by a spontaneous outburst of mirth from the entire audience, but that is what often happens. 'Crikey, the woman weighs a ton' isn't even mildly amusing, yet the Custard Factory audience exploded into their biggest laugh of the night. It echoed round the auditorium for quite some time, feeding on itself. Greatly to La Mancuna's credit (as I assured her later) she then sang her 'Wicked, wicked men' and 'Men are watching' lines with an elan that sent shivers running down my spine.

After the choir rehearsal scene the plot moved back to the original seaside town, where several disgraceful events took place. The very last scene of the show had Orla's pick-up from the Edinburgh bar – Stephen – arriving in the town by coach very early morning. The pair met and kissed chastely. Stephen had left his spectacles behind and Orla had abandoned her mouth brace. As planned, she took him onto the hillside overlooking the bay. In the half light they lay down on a tartan rug that Orla had brought along. Her mood was perky, considering that she'd felt her sickness returning, her period of remission from cancer at an end.

She asked the boy 'Do you believe in ghosts?'

'No', he said.

'You're with one now. Just for the night. That's why I'm good for you.

'Because you're a ghost?'

'Yes. You can do anything you want with me and that's what men wish for. It's a once-in-a-lifetime experience for you.'

The couple embraced. Amade's music flowed over them, conveying the unfathomable feelings of a dying girl on the verge of womanhood. The auditorium was utterly still and silent.

Every fibre of my being was focused on the scene, so I'd actually forgotten about the American submarine 'parked' out in the bay and Sharon's saying she hadn't the resources to depict it in motion. Suddenly the dark form of the sub – which I'd assumed was part of the painted backdrop – lit up against the early morning sky and we saw its conning tower driving towards the narrow inlet of the bay. How Sharon had achieved this effect I couldn't begin to guess, and I didn't want to know. It was enough to revel in the moment and to share in the mass intake of breath that rippled through the auditorium. The sublime orchestral score put a seal on the whole experience.

Sharon always said a successful show made an audience reluctant to leave the theatre. After the curtain calls and 'bravos', the wild applause and further curtain calls, we had the devil of a job shifting the buggers, who seemed disposed to linger all night. As people finally left the foyer they were met by a tout selling black market tickets, which must have indicated some measure of success.

Of course we were anxious to clear the stage and break open the crates of wine that were waiting patiently in the wings. The musicians laid down their instruments, singers scraped off their greasepaint, and the celebrations began.

The first thing I did was to quiz Sharon Adair about her change of heart.

'Sharon. The sub. You did it after all!'

She shrugged. 'Oh, you know. We had to get the thing out of the bay somehow.'

'I hope you haven't gone into the red. Because if so...'

'It's all right.' She nodded towards the figure of Amade. 'Martin wanted you to have it. He made a contribution.'

'What *do* you mean?'

She put one hand on her hip, a characteristic pose. 'Tell me, how many instrumentalists do you think were on stage?'

I hesitated. 'You said he could have twelve, didn't you?'

'There were ten. It was his contribution towards saving money.

What's money, anyway. You were right and so was he.'

We both turned to watch Amade as he larked about with two sopranos on the far side of the stage. He wasn't a man accustomed to attracting women but after such an evening, conscious of his own omnipotence, he moved amongst the company with a composed serenity. His expression, normally sober, brimmed with animation.

'He knows what he's achieved here,' Sharon murmured. 'Martin never writes for posterity on purpose, but he can't help himself. Come on, let's have a word.'

'We crossed to Amade and showered him with congratulations. He laughed and joked, but when Sharon said 'You'll actually make some money from this one,' he was momentarily more serious. 'Too much for what I did,' he said. 'Not enough for what I could do.'

It was time I pretended to be 'one of the boys'. I picked up a plate of canapés and moved about offering them to people. Eventually I came up against Stourage and La Mancuna, standing silently side by side, drawn together by talent and divided by temperament. There was just one canapé left on the plate.

'Why don't you finish it off?' said La Mancuna. 'I've heard that you always want the last one.'

Stourage smiled sweetly, like a vampire ready to strike. 'Oh no, you have it. You need to keep your strength up.'

Reference

(Ref 21) *We may guess the importance Bridger attached to this event, because a copy of 'The sopranos' playbill was attached to the relevant page of the diary.*

October 27, 2035

After success comes a period of uncertainty during which we all found it hard to settle. I was the fortunate one, having several rubbish scripts to work on which can't be damaged however much I blunder. Amade fared worse, according to Connie. The effort demanded by *The sopranos* left him in listless mood. Added to that, he is clearly unwell. He suffered from a new pain in his hands and a familiar one in the lower body that his 'useless quack' (Connie's phrase) was powerless to locate. He has vomited on several occasions. There was mental anguish too; with *The sopranos* over, Amade's thoughts were increasingly haunted by his wife's *bête noire*, the vampire oratorio.

In a dismal mood this evening I've been thinking about Amade and trying to visualise his features. I wish I'd kept a photograph of the man. The 2020s fashion for taking 'selfies' – which swept the world in a torrent of narcissism – has died down in 2035. There's been a reaction against it, which is no doubt why I've never raised a camera in Amade's direction. He isn't a man whose physical presence causes people in the street to turn and look; far from it. He is short in stature and has recently become quite podgy. But as with anyone else it is Amade's face that gives the key to his personality. My pet theory is that few of history's great men and women would stand out in a crowd. I do not believe Shakespeare's features – from the little we know of them – would attract attention. With the giants it is their deeds that make them memorable. Secure in the knowledge of their own genius, they do not feel the need to impress.

If there is one quality that defines Amade it is that of melancholy. It emanates from his person as a strong perfume does from some women. He doesn't exactly wallow in misery, but will remark in a conversational tone 'You know, I think of death every living day'. It knocks you back a bit. He told me once that death, when we consider it closely, is the true god of our existence; that he'd formed a close relationship with this the best and truest friend of mankind, so that its image was no longer terrifying to him but soothing and consoling. It is this pattern of thought that explains Amade's ever-pensive expression. No doubt it also accounts for the potency of his best compositions.

Of course melancholy doesn't rule out Amade's more capricious moods. According to Connie he could in his youth be very silly indeed. The first day I set eyes on the man was in a Birmingham street, where he played the clown with friends, yapping like a dog and cocking his leg against a lamp-post. You could say he is like a child, capable of a child's silliness but also a child's piercing honesty. I have come to know these qualities and to value them dearly.

November 10, 2035

A worrying morning. Amade's custom is to take a morning constitutional, walking from his house into the centre of Moseley. He says the rhythms of a walk help to put his thoughts in order, and I've seen him stop en route to take a notebook from his pocket to jot down ideas for a composition. This daily perambulation is precisely timed – 'You can set your watch to it', Connie says – and I'm in the habit of joining him now and then; not walking, god forbid, but taking a bus and tracking the man down to one of his usual haunts. He seems pleased enough to see me, or at least to tolerate my company; I hope so, anyway. Sometimes we'll try out one of the alternative-type cafés still to be found in Moseley, but more often we'll sit on a wooden bench near the ancient gents toilet, situated on a triangular patch of grass that hasn't experienced a mower's blade for many moons. We sit there knee-deep in plant life, near two or three hobos who lie on ground-sheets under scraps of canvas, and Amade will scatter some coins in their direction. He is known in the area and well regarded, a source of local pride.

This morning's experience was different from any that had preceded it. Arriving in Moseley at the usual time I could see no sign of my friend. I tried the obvious places, then retired to our bench and sat wrapped in my own thoughts, in the company of several of the usual tramp-like figures sprawled about. Knowing Amade's schedule, I felt sure now that he wouldn't turn up. In this I was wrong, for twenty minutes later – an eternity in Amade-time – I saw his familiar figure approaching. That is, familiar and not familiar. He was using a stick, which I'd not been aware of before, and moved with painful slowness, staring ahead like a sightless man. Reaching the bench he made a gesture of recognition but did not speak, then sat heavily. At his feet a bearded man with his flies undone was cradling a bottle of cider under one arm.

'Good morning, Mr Amade.'

Amade groped in his pocket for money but seemed unable to extract the coins. A pantomime of this fumbling seemed to go on for an eternity. In my embarrassment I broke the habit of a lifetime, and to the beardy's evident surprise handed over some cash. The man levered himself up onto one elbow and spoke again.

'How are you, Mr Amade sir? I do hope you are in good health. I wish you well, sir. We all do.'

Amade is a man of surprises After a rest he rallied and managed to walk home again, though I trailed him all the way. The incident troubled me. I've seen him fall ill before and recover sufficiently to pen a work of genius, so I have to believe he can do it again. I refuse to contemplate the unthinkable.

November 20, 2035

Connie buzzed me early this morning. It was unusual, and I knew something had to be very wrong. She was crying and her voice reached me indistinctly. The preceding evening Amade had asked her to walk with him, and they went to a park near their house. The sun was shining and the pair of them sat on a bench next to some flower beds. She said all this. Amade told her that he felt empty and had no reason to live. 'Everything is cold as ice,' was the expression he used. He said that he knew he could not last much longer; that he could feel his strength ebbing; that it was an irony this happened just as they had a little money for once, with the success of *Sopranos* and the unexpected windfall from the oratorio; that in writing the oratorio he was writing to mark his own death. Connie pleaded with him but Amade assured her he was finished. Now she's taken the oratorio away from him to 'curb its malign influence,' as she put it. This alone signals how far Amade has declined; until recently Connie wouldn't have dared to interfere in his work. Now Amade's strength is passing to her, and I believe she can sustain it. But of course nobody – nobody in the world – can compose as Amade does. I have come late to that understanding. Events rush upon us and there is barely time even for regret.

November 23, 2035

This morning I rose earlier than usual and went into Moseley by bus, arriving at a time that should have meshed with Amade's walking routine. I'd been told that he was still active and still composing. Even so my actions were irrational. I felt strangely impelled into Moseley, as if failing to be at the spot where he and I sometimes met meant that he couldn't get there. I was not thinking straight.

The little area with the benches and the long grass and the lolling winos was unchanged. I stood there a while, knowing he wouldn't come. It struck me that the sunny weather, so rarely seen these days, had been sent to mock Amade's condition. I wasn't thinking straight.

After a bit I turned away and ought to have gone home. Instead my feet instinctively retraced the route that Amade always took. It wasn't long before I turned a corner and saw him. Next to the main road was a ramshackle enterprise that specialised in garden furniture and metal sculptures, examples of which were displayed across 20 yards of pavement. Amade was on a bench with a metal sculpture of the sun on one side and a strutting peacock on the other. I hurried to greet him, to say how pleased I was to see him out and about, but he couldn't manage a reply. He raised a feeble hand and grasped my fingers.

I told him 'Come on, old friend. I'll take you home.'

With help he rose, but his weight was heavy on my arm and his feet barely moved. Someone called my name and I saw Connie scurrying towards us. We took an arm each and moved at a funereal pace towards the house. In their living room Connie had set up a bed next to the piano; from it Amade would be able to reach out and touch the keys. The mother-in-law materialised, a little ray of sunshine (as ever), and I made myself scarce so the two women could prepare him for bed. I waved goodbye at the doorway and wondered if he would ever leave that bed again.

November 30, 2035

I was right about Amade not leaving his bed and wish I hadn't been. A week has passed since I helped him to get home. He is conscious but his condition worsens. Low spirits are a big part of it. Connie keeps me informed and says she can see no hope for him.

Since the illness began we've endured the most extraordinary spell of weather. I barely know how to describe it on paper. The sky has been almost black, unrelieved by clouds and certainly by sunshine. Rain falls steadily, a heavy unceasing deluge with no particular character except its remorseless nature. In my lodgings we hear the drumming of water on the roof 24 hours a day. None of us can remember anything like it; a medieval society would be talking about the end of the world. The streets are alive with water and the railway line is flooded. On the canal a longboat has broken free of its moorings and become wedged in the brickwork of the bridge. Of course it would be fanciful to ascribe the deluge to Amade's impending death, but it cannot be a favourable omen for life.

When nothing can be done for someone, people redouble their efforts. I've just made the trip into Moseley, mostly for Connie's sake; some foodstuffs that she probably won't eat. People say she doesn't care, that she's always away from home, but nobody could be more broken by the illness of a partner. The tears never stop, spraying her haggard face. Her cracked voice could be coming from a woman on the verge of insanity.

On arriving at the house I'd been astonished to find people outside on the pavement. They stood in the rain not expecting good news or bad, offering support by their silent presence. They came and went, but overall the numbers increased. It astonishes me now that the first time I heard Amade's music his name was unknown to me. It seems the same cannot be said of his neighbours.

December 2, 2035

Still this ghastly weather goes on. Friends say I'm being ridiculous, but I've convinced myself that there will be no let-up until Amade is dead.

I went to Moseley again today, finding it hard to stay away. Connie let me in and I was shocked by her appearance. The doctor had just left and she was glad to be shot of 'His Uselessness' (her regular descriptor). He'd spoken of hospital, but that was merely going through the motions. There are no beds available and Amade has no wish to go. It would be cruel to move a man in his condition, paralysed down one side. They are all waiting for the end.

Nancy Stourage called while I was there. Whatever the girl's shortcomings, she has been constant in her devotion to Amade. Connie seized her chance and persuaded Stourage to sing to the dying man, something he has repeatedly asked for. What did he want to hear? Of course it had to be the vampire oratorio. Amade continues to brood about the piece and occasionally tries to sing a phrase from the score, which Connie is able to identify despite the hoarseness of his voice. It was strange for me to see – a first – Connie accompanying on the piano, quite creditably, though I knew that every wrong note would cause Amade distress. Stourage had chosen the section where Harker's fiancée broods upon the cause of her sickness. It is ineffably sad under any circumstances and we were all in tears by the end. Amade's expression was hard to read, which was just as well. The mystery of the oratorio's genesis – the dark messenger, and all that – hasn't helped his condition one bit. I wonder now if that will ever be cleared up. (**Ref 22**)

Reference

(Ref 22) Some time after Amade's death the origins of the oratorio did come to light. The story is an odd one. A London businessman who made a fortune from shoes was also a music fanatic. He had the unusual custom of anonymously commissioning pieces from known composers. In a few instances he would allow friends to think that he was the composer. Most of what the man did was harmless enough but in this case, coinciding as it did with Amade's illness, the results were unfortunate. The silver lining is that we have an oratorio, albeit an incomplete one.

December 5, 2035

Well it's over, and I'm glad. Glad for Connie and all who knew the man and above all glad for Amade, whose suffering over the past two weeks must have been intolerable.

It's weird but I was almost there at the moment of his death. How to explain the sense of a gathering crisis when someone is very ill? I'd felt it all week, and late yesterday evening simply had to walk out of my lodgings and make for Moseley. I got a different bus from my usual which took me two-thirds of the way, and walked the rest. The rain came down, as it has done for so long; within minutes I was very wet.

Outside his house there were more people than ever, but far from standing silently they were shuffling about in agitation. Before I could ask anyone, the reason became clear. From an open window came the sound of a woman screaming in the most demented fashion. It contrasted horribly with the first time I'd been to the house and heard the limpid sound of Nancy Stourage's soprano drifting from a window.

I ran to the front door and pummelled with my fists. It opened to reveal the mother-in-law, who for the first time ever actually spoke to me.

'Come quickly, she's lost all reason. Hurry, damn you, hurry.'

She moved like a cat into their living room and I trailed after her. What met my eyes there was something I shall never forget. The bed stood in the same position next to the piano. Amade's face was on the pillow with all the life drained from it. The sheets were thrown back revealing the foul evidence of vomit and other effluents around the corpse. The stench was indescribable. In amongst all this Connie clung to the body of her dead husband shrieking like a lost soul. If her words meant anything she was saying she wanted to go with him. The hellish vision contrasted with Connie's usually controlled demeanour.

Another woman in the room, whom I recognised as Connie's sister

Sophie, was tugging ineffectually at her sibling's arm. I said that if she would run the shower in the bathroom I'd get her sister there. That is what happened, although Connie resisted like a maniac along the way. Once under hot water she quietened down a bit, and I left them to it. The sisters got on well enough under normal circumstances.

I went back out to the front and told the waiting people what had happened. As I used the words 'Amade dead' a heart-rending sigh came from the company, a sound of grief and sympathy and acceptance that might have given Connie some relief if she'd heard it. The people embraced and comforted each other but were reluctant to leave the scene, notwithstanding the unremitting rain.

Back in the house I buzzed the morgue to come for Amade's body, then went to help the mother-in-law with the horror-scene of the bed. The old woman kept reiterating the words 'fifty-five', until I understood that Amade had died at fifty-five minutes past midnight; it seemed to be important to her. Having ignored me for months, she was now talking the hind legs off a donkey. She said Stourage had been at the house earlier and Amade told her "Come back tonight, Nancy, and see me die".' She seemed resentful that Amade had vouchsafed these sentiments to Stourage rather than the close family. Did she even like her illustrious son-in-law? I had no idea. Still she banged on. According to her Amade told Stourage 'I have the taste of death on my tongue.'

We cleaned up Amade's body as best we could, waiting on the arrival of the morgue transport. Sophie had put Connie to bed, where she fell into a turbulent sleep. I'm afraid I complied when Sophie urged me to go home; the atmosphere of that house was one any sane man would want to leave behind.

I went out past the handful of people who still lingered in the street and started for my lodgings. The rain came down. There was no chance of transport at that hour and walking in the small hours is a risky business, but I felt glad to put one foot before the other and keep personal thoughts at bay. I wanted not to think about loss; I don't mean my loss, but everyone's loss.

December 9, 2035

Amade's funeral took place four days after his death. We mourners gathered at the house waiting for the hearse to arrive from the morgue. After two horrendous weeks the weather was preparing itself for a spectacular climax, and people had long passed the point of expecting to be dry.

Such is the affection for Amade locally that well-wishers still gathered in the street. Yet the company within the Amade household was pitifully small. There were just four relatives, including a sadly diminished Connie and the mother-in-law (who had renewed her vow of silence). Sharon Adair was there, and Stourage of course, plus another singer. The unexpected presence was Manas Chatterji, who had surprisingly made the pilgrimage from Alum Rock. La Mancuna, no; she'd set aside the morning to have her nails painted.

A telegram had been sent by Joseph Hagen from Germany and – astonishingly, given the state of our postal service – had arrived without causing any complications. (A local saying is 'If you have an enemy, send him a telegram'.)

As we waited for the hearse the conversation was restrained, in deference to Connie's low spirits. Only the singer – a bass who'd taken a minor part in *The Sopranos* toilet scene – was in talkative mood. He cornered me in the kitchen to expound his views.

'Of course there is no doubt about Amade's genius,' he declared.

'All the more reason for us to mourn his early demise,' I replied. 'We could have hoped for many more years of such a great talent. It's such a tragic loss!'

'I'm not so sure.' The singer, put his finger-tips together like someone performing in a debating chamber; god he was irritating. 'Do you not think that our dear Amade was like a hot-house plant, brought too early to a state of perfection. We have had all we can possibly expect from that source.'

I looked around, hoping Connie wasn't within earshot. Manas Chatterji, the only other person present, was shaking his head, and actually said 'No'.

The singer was affronted. 'What do you mean, no?'

'He means you're talking a load of bollocks,' I told him. 'Please keep your views to yourself, especially when Amade's wife is within hearing.'

Fortunately the funeral party arrived to preclude further conversation, and we all moved towards the door. Out in the street were two vehicles – the hearse, and a limousine big enough to take all the mourners. Both very basic-looking affairs, much the worse for wear. The hearse contained just the cane coffin (a 'creak, squeak and leak,' affair, as they've become known). No flowers. The employee in charge of this sad cavalcade looked distinctly on the rough side, which was hardly surprising. Connie had insisted on keeping down the costs of burial. Amade's death, just as he'd begun earning decent money, had removed all means of support from her, and she was grey with financial worry on top of personal grief. In fact (I don't know what came over me) it was me who forked out for the limousine, on the strict understanding that she didn't tell anyone. Our funeral party was destined for the nearest Catholic cemetery, a 45-minute drive away. Connie had refused the services of a priest ('None of that mumbo jumbo, thank you') and settled for an informal gathering round the graveside.

We piled into the limousine and the two vehicles moved slowly away down the street, past the ranks of local people standing heads bowed at the roadside. I was profoundly glad not to be driving in the prevailing conditions. The downpour was so intense that visibility cannot have been more than a few yards. We dragged along at a pitiful pace, the passengers strangely silent, the only sound that of rain on the roof.

After 20 minutes the limousine's engine broke down, and the vehicle rolled to a stop at the roadside. Sharon Adair wound down a window and found we were in a nondescript rural area. The hearse had moved on out of sight and showed no signs of returning. I felt sorry for our driver who had to get out and throw back the bonnet, looking in vain for the source of the trouble. He soon gave up and returned, very wet, to buzz his HQ. Half an hour later an engineer arrived and with commendable speed got the limousine going again.

A cause for concern was that the limousine driver had lost phone contact with his colleague in the other vehicle. We finally arrived at the cemetery – an utterly desolate scene, with rain sweeping across a waterlogged landscape – and found no trace of the hearse. Out went the poor driver again and found two cemetery workers in a wooden hut. They confirmed that our hearse had been there and had lowered the cane coffin into one of the new plots. Unfortunately two other coffins arrived during the same period and the men were unable to confirm which patch of fresh earth was Amade's. The bass singer suggested we choose a plot at random and gather round to 'say a few words'. No-one fancied this, least of all Connie. She turned in the front seat, grey-faced, barely conscious, Sophie's arm solicitously round her shoulders, to apologise for what had happened.

Manas Chatterji spoke up from the back of the vehicle. 'Please Mrs Amade, do not trouble yourself in the least bit. The worst that can happen had already happened. Forgive me, but when all is said and done the whereabouts of Mr Amade's mortal remains are of little account. It is the glory of his life and work that will always be with us Do not upset yourself, I beg you'.

There were murmurs of agreement, and the limousine turned round to take us back into Birmingham. Amade's brief existence on this earth had run its course (**Ref 23**)

Reference

(Ref 23) *It is good to have this account of the events at Amade's funeral. It contradicts the legend that has grown up: that Amade was buried in an unmarked grave because the mourners – his wife in particular – couldn't be troubled to accompany the hearse to the burial ground.*

December 20, 2035

Two weeks have passed since Amade's funeral. I'm concerned about Connie – who is left with no source of income – but I hesitate to intrude upon private grief. I sent her a couple of short notes affirming my support. Then this morning she buzzed and asked me to go round. 'I have news,' she said, but wouldn't be drawn further.

It seemed odd to be walking down her road in dry weather, the tempest having lifted soon after Amade's body was consigned to the earth. Odd too to have the feeling that I would find *him* at home, whilst knowing full well that was impossible. Of course the neighbourhood was back to normal; no mourners lining the pavements. Things move on, as they have to.

Connie opened the door to me. She was subdued, but the old lift of the shoulders and the bustling movement had returned, I was very glad to see. She appeared to have the house to herself. As I'd expected, Amade's absence was palpable; he'd always been present when I visited before.

She provided coffee, and I handed over some obituaries taken from online. We sat on the sofa near the piano.

'You look OK,' I ventured.

'I was off my head, silly woman. I've recovered a semblance of sanity.'

'It was understandable Connie, with all the horrible stuff that happened. And I know you're worried about the future. It's so difficult to make any kind of income these days. If I can be of any...'

'That's what I wanted to tell you,' she broke in, rising from the sofa. Come and have a look.'

She led me across the room and pointed to an old trunk that stood under the window. I was vaguely aware of its former existence, when it had been covered with a rug.

She kicked the trunk. 'This stupid thing carried a lot of household junk when we arrived in the house. We emptied it and just left it here in the living room.'

'And...' Where was she was going with this?

'Open it, why don't you. Have a look.'

The 'stupid thing' wasn't locked, so I bent down and flung back the lid.

'And hey presto,' cried Connie.

Inside, the chest was chock full of papers. I saw immediately that they were all covered with hieroglyphics in Amade's hand, the fruits of musical composition. Crochets, minims, semi-quavers, hundreds and thousands of notes sprawling untidily across the bits of paper as Amade's fingers had struggled to keep pace with the workings of his mind. I put a hand into the trunk and idly stirred the contents around. I saw lined paper, blank paper, stapled foolscap sheets, proper composition paper with neatly ruled staves, old envelopes, scraps of newspaper, a discarded shopping list, all of them decorated with Amade's madcap inventions.

'*Four years*,' said Connie. 'The longest time we've stayed anywhere. Four years of work.'

'So...so he...'

'I always told him,' she cried, passionately, 'Write it down. I always said.'

'Not that you were a nagging wife, of course.'

'Are you kidding. Of course I fucking nagged. What are wives for? I knew. I knew he needed to organise the work. That creative part of him, it spilled out beyond any control. I'd hear the piano going like the clappers, Martin's godawful singing...no way could *I* record it and there was no-one else.'

'Yet all the time...'

'Yes, somehow, some time...when I was tucked up in bed maybe, doing to myself what he ought to have been doing, he *was* writing it all down...it's...' She too delved into the trunk and stirred the paper sludge.

'It's a treasure trove.'

'Yes.' She sat down again, calmer. 'I really believe it is. And luckily, I'm the one who can decipher all this, even if doing it will finally drive me over the edge.'

'You know what this means better than anyone,' I said. 'Amade's reputation is growing so fast...well you saw them standing out in the rain. Even in Alum Rock I saw it. They love him. They adore him.'

'Oh yes – try being married to him.'

'Four years of new music, it'll make all the difference. Hell, there's no limit. He'll become a household name...'

'He will if I have anything to do with it.'

There wasn't much more for us to say and not long afterwards she accompanied me to the front door, as she had the first time I visited the house, months before. We said our goodbyes.

Maybe it was the expression on her face, or the way she stood slightly closer than usual, but I swear we both had the same thought running through our minds. Of course it would have been all wrong – not that that's ever stopped me before; perhaps I'm becoming wiser with age. I leaned over to plant a chaste kiss on her forehead, then stepped out into the road. **(Ref 24)**

Reference

(Ref 24) Bridger's diary ends abruptly here. It seems unlikely that at the start of it he intended to focus so much on Amade, but it is how things turned out and posterity will be grateful. The diary contains clarifications of various points that have long puzzled Amade experts. Leaving the historical record aspects to one side, I believe Bridger's account is also a good read in its own right. How far can it be trusted? The scholars I've shown it to reckon that the contents are likely to be 90% accurate.

Editor's note

Martin Amade has been my constant companion for the past few months and I hope I may be forgiven for describing a recent experience that relates to him. I had spent an afternoon working in London's Sloane Square, and afterwards needed to get to Victoria Station. Unusually, I felt like walking. It is ill-advised these days for a woman on her own, but I was wearing trousers and unisex headgear and needed the exercise. I turned into Pimlico Road and went east to the junction with Ebury Street, where I chanced upon a small square that had clearly seen better times.

I had resolved not to linger, so as to avoid any trouble, and was turning north towards Victoria when I spotted a plinth that had once supported some kind of statue. All that remained of its former subject was part of one foot, a sadly familiar circumstance with London statues, which have been vandalised on a grand scale. However the plinth had survived in its entirety; a circular structure about four feet high with a metal railing around the perimeter.

Dusk was descending, but there was enough light to see some kind of design on the outside of the plinth. Nobody was about, which encouraged me to take a closer look. A single design went 360 degrees round the entire base. Against a dark background were fragmented elements of musicians and musical instruments that clearly suggested an orchestra: a hand held a violin bow; a woman's lips fastened upon a woodwind instrument; a shadowy figure stood behind a set of kettle drums; and so on. There was no inscription. I am no judge of art but I thought the painting had been superbly executed.

The faces in the picture were all turned in the same direction. They were looking at the unmistakable figure of a conductor with baton in hand. To my amazement it was immediately evident that this person was Martin Amade; the bunch of hair at his neck, the reflective, almost tormented expression left no doubt. Martin Amade.

By now the light was fading rapidly. I got out my phone and took some photographs, feeling a sense of astonishment and wonder. For *five months* I had worked on Bridger's diary without finding any reference to a portrait of Martin Amade in London. What was it doing there? Who would trouble to make such a thing when vandals could come along and smash the work to pieces? From memory I dredged up the name of a phantom open-air painter called Banksy who had been active 40 years earlier and whose style – I recalled – was similar to what I now saw. There had been some mystery about Banksy's identity and I believe there were rumours about a son who continued his father's work. Banksy could not possibly be alive now, but a son...? It seemed highly unlikely.

Other questions abounded. Why had I heard nothing about this painting? Could it perhaps be a very recent work? Could I even be (moving now into the world of fantasy) one of the first people to set eyes on it? And above all why a painting of Amade just here, on this anonymous little plinth in the middle of nowhere?

I can only record what I saw. I assume the artist, whoever it was, felt strongly enough about Martin Amade to pay this worthy if ephemeral tribute. I have put my photos of the painting into the edition of Bridger's diary and left open the matter of their attribution. Perhaps in time that question will be resolved.

Kate Temple, 2066

Sources

H C Robbins Landon. *1791: Mozart's last year.* Flamingo, 2nd ed. 1989.

Alfred Einstein. *Mozart: his character – his work.* Panther Arts, 1971.

Eric Blom. *Mozart.* Dent, 1962.

Mozart's letters, edited and introduced by Eric Blom, selected from The letters of Mozart and his family, translated and annotated by Emily Anderson. Penguin Books, 1956.

Mozart's letters, Mozart's life: selected letters, edited and newly translated by Robert Spaethling. Faber, 2000.

Sheila Hodges. *Lorenzo da Ponte: The life and times of Mozart's librettist.* University of Wisconsin Press, 2002. Rodney Bolt. *Lorenzo da Ponte: The adventures of Mozart's librettist in the old and new worlds.* Bloomsbury, 2007.

Alan Warner. *The sopranos.* Vintage, 1999.

Printed in Great Britain
by Amazon